ICE

SAN JUAN SHADOWS - BOOK 2

Lynnette BONNER

ICE
SAN JUAN SHADOWS, Book 2

Published by Pacific Lights Publishing
Copyright © 2020 by Lynnette Bonner. All rights reserved.

Cover design by Lynnette Bonner of Indie Cover Design, images ©
    www.depositphotos.com, File: #1262186_ds - Ice
    www.depositphotos.com, File: # 3485589_ds - Boat
    www.depositphotos.com, File: #43163769_ds - Woman0
eBook design by Jon Stewart of Stewart Design

Scriptures taken from the Holy Bible, New International Version®, NIV®. Copyright © 1973, 1978, 1984, 2011 by Biblica, Inc.™ Used by permission of Zondervan. All rights reserved worldwide. www.zondervan.com The "NIV" and "New International Version" are trademarks registered in the United States Patent and Trademark Office by Biblica, Inc.™

ISBN: 978-1-942982-17-3

Ice is a work of fiction. References to real people, events, establishments, organizations, or locales are intended only to provide a sense of authenticity and are used fictitiously. All other characters, incidents, and dialogue are drawn from the author's imagination.

OTHER CONTEMPORARY BOOKS
BY LYNNETTE BONNER

THE PACIFIC SHORES SERIES
Contemporary Romance

Beyond the Waves - BOOK ONE
Caught in the Current - BOOK TWO
Song of the Surf - BOOK THREE
Written in the Sand - BOOK FOUR

THE ISLANDS OF INTRIGUE SERIES
Contemporary Romantic Suspense

The Unrelenting Tide - BOOK ONE
(There are more books in this series by other authors.)

THE RIVERSONG SERIES
Contemporary Romance

Angel Kisses and Riversong - BOOK ONE
Soft Kisses and Birdsong - BOOK TWO

Find all other books by Lynnette Bonner at:
www.lynnettebonner.com

*But seek first his kingdom and his righteousness,
and all these things will be given to you as well.
Therefore do not worry about tomorrow,
for tomorrow will worry about itself.
Each day has enough trouble of its own.*

Matthew 6: 33 & 34 NIV

Chapter 1

Camryn Hunt's feet ached as she stepped onto the darkened Everett street in front of D & J's Diner and trudged toward the bus stop. She glanced at her watch. Five after ten, already? It had been a long day. Twelve-hour shifts were all well and good if you sat behind a desk. But hauling around trays full of heavy plated-meals for twelve hours was simply exhausting.

At least she had a job. After the chaos the Coronavirus inflicted on the economy, she was thankful to have work at all. Hopefully, she'd be able to get another car soon—she'd lost hers when she was laid off from her teaching assistant position when all the schools had closed down for the year. But for now, she chose to be thankful for public transportation—and that though it was completely dark, the streets in this part of town were well lit.

Washington's public transportation was at least saving her from another monthly payment. Her gut crimped at the thought of her bills. When she'd been in school, taking out loans had seemed like the smart thing to do. It had allowed her to study more and get better grades. But now that her payments had started coming due, she wasn't sure how she was going to keep ahead of everything. Even though she lived in a tiny studio apartment, her desire to live in a safe neighborhood of the city made her rent almost astronomical. Plus, she had to pay for water and garbage.

Before her mother passed, she'd needed a private-care home. Mom had no insurance other than Medicare, which didn't cover all the costs. For months Camryn had been able to keep up with the other portion of the payment, despite being in school, but then she'd lost her job. Thankfully, the care provider had been understanding of her situation. He offered to continue the care, with the understanding that she would begin making payments on what was owed as soon as she could or within twelve months of care-termination, whichever came first. Mom had passed away, but not before racking up fifteen thousand dollars of care costs. The end of the twelve-month grace period was in two weeks. And she truly did want to pay the man. He'd been more than generous. He'd cared for Mom for six months with only partial pay before she passed.

Camryn sighed and glanced toward the sky. She might pray if she thought it would change anything. It wasn't that she didn't believe in God. She just wasn't sure that she was important enough for Him to bother with. But maybe that was simply the result of living through a back-to-back string of extremely lousy months.

Losing Mom had been the biggest blow of all. She was alone in the world now. But God didn't seem to care much about that either. For a while she'd prayed that the right man would come into her life. But after a series of Mr. Wrongs, she'd given up on that prayer too.

An icy wind danced down the street and slipped fingers around her neck. She tucked her coat closer about her throat with one hand and adjusted the cross-body strap of her purse with the other as she rounded the corner onto Hewitt. She eyed the bench at the bus stop ahead with gratefulness. It would be the first time she had sat down since the fifteen-minute break she'd squeezed in for lunch. The bus wasn't due to arrive for another ten minutes. She only hoped she'd still be awake when it pulled up. But the chill in the air ought to help with that. She never could sleep when she was cold.

On the opposite side of the street, a shadowy figure in a gray hoodie darted from the entrance of the Everpark Garage.

Camryn pressed a hand to her chest and squinted into the depths of the garage, trying to see what he might be running from, but the concealing shadows cast by the streetlights were too heavy. She couldn't make out anything except a brief glow of an orange dot.

She returned her focus to the hooded man.

Not bothering to get to the crosswalk, he gave a cursory check in both directions, then dashed toward her side of the street.

Camryn hesitated, caution rising further. Should she be afraid of him? One could never be too careful, yet the man wasn't even looking in her direction.

Tires squealed, jerking her focus a little farther up the block. She leaned forward to peer between the edge of the bus stop shelter and the leafless branches of a potted tree which stood between her and the street.

A car careened around the corner, coming from the far side of the parking garage. Headlights blinded her for a moment. With a gasp, she realized the running man was silhouetted in the glare.

"Dear God!"

He was going to get hit!

"Watch out!"

Her hand dropped automatically to her phone in the apron pocket of her uniform. She heard the fleeing man yelp, then the ghastly sound of impact. He tumbled across the hood. Rocketed up the windshield. Crested the roof. For a horrifying instant, he was airborne, and then he crashed to the pavement with a grunt.

The coupe hesitated, headlights pointing directly at her.

One hand clutching her phone, Camryn held up her other to squint past the glare toward the man in the road.

The screech of rubber fighting for grip on pavement pierced the night once more. The car fishtailed before it leapt toward her.

For one heart-jolting moment, Camryn thought the car would jump the curb. She lurched further behind the flimsy protection of the plexiglass-encased bus stop. But the vehicle kept to the street. It peeled out and zipped past her in a blur.

Camryn felt her stomach curl.

A bald man in the passenger seat had been holding up a phone, obviously taking a video of her. Why would he be doing that when the driver had just run somebody over? Was this some sort of terrible social-media challenge? Kill someone while live-streaming?

One red taillight glowered through the night as the car screeched around the corner at the next block and disappeared from sight, leaving a great billow of smoke obscuring the entire area.

Camryn shook her head and swiped at the clouds of burnt rubber. She left the shelter and dashed forward on trembling legs. Her fingers shook as she fumbled to dial 911 and run towards the moaning man in the street at the same time.

"Sir, are you alright?" She gritted her teeth. It was a stupid question. She poked the speakerphone button and set her phone on the pavement as she fell to her knees by his side. Her hands fluttered over him. Even in the light of the streetlamps, she could see that his clothes and every exposed patch of dark skin were slick with blood. "Dear Jesus." One of his legs canted at an odd angle behind him. The man rolled his head from side to side, groaning in anguish.

"I'm so sorry. Where does it hurt?" Another stupid question. By the sight of him, he probably hurt everywhere.

"Nine-one-one what is your emergency?"

"A-a man was j-just run over by a car." She needed to get a grip. But she only seemed able to breathe in choppy bursts.

"Where are you, ma'am?"

Of course, she should have said that first. But her mind was blank. Camryn squinted at the street sign. It was too far away to read. *Think.* "Uh...I'm near the Everpark Garage. Out front."

A keyboard clicked in the background. "I see an Everpark on Hewitt, ma'am. Is that the one?"

"Yes!" It was as if that bit of information had blown away all the clouds obscuring her street-name recall. "Hewitt Avenue. Between Colby and Hoyt."

"And you said a man was run over by a car? Is he alive?"

"Yes. He's moving. But there's lots of blood. I don't want to hurt him worse."

"Okay, ma'am, I need you to stay calm and stay with me on the phone. Help is on the way. What's your name?"

"Camryn. Camryn Hunt."

"Are you in danger, Camryn?"

A chill zipped down her spine. She lifted her head to scan the street and was surprised to see several bystanders gathering along the sidewalks. What if the driver came back? But the street remained empty, and with witnesses now looking on, it wasn't likely anyone would do anything to her. "I-I don't think so. The car drove off."

The injured man clutched for her, tugging at her jacket with one hand, and she suddenly realized he was murmuring something. But the 911 operator was also asking another question. Camryn ignored the phone and scooted closer to the man's head. She leaned over him so she could look him right in the eyes. "What is it? Tell me what you need."

His mouth opened and shut a couple times, and she could hear a sickening bubbly sound at the back of his throat. Without thinking, she gently pried his hand from her jacket. His fingers tangled in the material for a moment, but then she was able to take them in her own. "I'm right here. I'm not leaving you until the paramedics get here. Help is on the way."

He gave a little shake of his head and blinked hard a couple times like he was trying to focus on her but was having trouble. "Pocket." He gritted. "Get it."

Camryn searched the length of him. His shirt had a pocket. She patted it, but it was empty. Then she noticed the man's free hand, which was mangled and torn, jabbing at the front right pocket of his unzipped hoodie.

His eyes widened with intensity. "Get it."

Camryn felt a hard rectangle through the fabric of the pocket. "This?" She pulled out a mangled iPhone. The poor man probably wanted to call his family. "I'm afraid it's broken, but you can use mine. What number do you want to call?" She reached for her phone even as she realized the 911 operator was speaking.

"Camryn, please don't hang up the phone!"

Camryn pressed her phone to her ear, forgetting for a moment that it was on speaker. "I think he wants to make a call, but his phone is smashed."

The man shook his head, and the hand she was still holding squeezed hers with surprising strength. His gaze drilled into hers intently. "No call. Pack. Police."

"Yes. I've already called 911. Help is on the way."

The man shook his head again. "Give. Phone. Pack. Po-lice." The words emerged in little moans.

Understanding dawned. She eyed the mangled bit of broken glass and bent metal. "You want me to give your phone to the police?"

He loosed a garbled breath. "Pack."

"Pack police." She had no idea what that meant.

The poor man seemed to relax a little. "Yes."

"I'll do it right away when they get here."

"Thank—" a breath slipped free and his head slumped to one side.

A hard knot formed in Camryn's chest. "Sir?" She gently shook his shoulder.

"Camryn, what's happening?" the dispatcher asked.

"I think he just died." Camryn sucked for oxygen. "I didn't even ask his name."

"Listen to me, Camryn. Do you know how to do CPR?"

"Y-yes." She'd had CPR training for her college lifeguard job. "But I've never had to do it."

"That's okay. I'm going to walk you through it. All you have to do is press on his chest fast and hard, okay? Remember mid-sternum. Not lower. Put the phone on speaker and set it down."

"It's already on speaker." She set her phone back on the pavement and shoved the man's phone into the pocket of her apron.

"Good. Now place your hands directly over his sternum. The smooth bone in the middle of his chest."

Camryn was already leaning over the man. In the distance, she heard the first notes of sirens. She automatically placed her hands, one atop the other, over his chest and stiffened her arms as she started pumping. "I can hear the sirens."

"Yes. That's good. I need you to pump his chest, Camryn. Nice and firm, but not too hard. Are you pumping?"

"I'm pumping."

Behind her, tires squealed and the bright glare of headlights slashed through the night.

Chapter 2

Island County Sheriff, Holden Parker, pulled his cruiser over to the curb in front of old Mrs. Hutchinson's San Juan Island house and cut the lights. She had a halogen porch light reminiscent of a prison yard. Through the branches of her now-dormant rose bushes, he could already see her waving her cane as she bellowed at Mr. Snowden, her next-door neighbor. The old coot was simply standing there, arms folded, but he wore that self-satisfied smile Holden had seen on him a thousand times.

Holden chuckled. He keyed his mic and let the Friday Harbor Office know that he'd arrived on the scene.

Dealing with the almost-without-fail, twice-weekly dispute between these two neighbors had become something of a joke down at headquarters. Island policing might not offer all the adrenaline and challenges that his Seattle homicide job had, but he would take this peacekeeping, kitten-rescuing position any day over trying to determine which suspect had offed a little girl or mother or husband.

Still, these two usually had their row much earlier in the day than this.

He climbed from behind the wheel, tamping his Stetson into place. The song of waves caressing the shore on the other side of these houses greeted him. "Mrs. Hutchinson, Mr. Snowden. What seems to be the problem tonight?" He reached automatically for his flashlight, then realized the porch light made it unnecessary.

For being almost eighty, Mrs. Hutchinson was as spry as a kid goat. She spun toward him, still swinging her cane, and about took his head off.

Holden leapt back. "Whoa there, ma'am."

She thumped the tip of her cane on the walk and advanced on him, stabbing an accusatory finger in Mr. Snowden's direction. "His filthy dog"—she spat the word like an epithet—"tinkled on my lawn again. And poor Miss Bluebell is now terrified to come into the yard because she can smell dog pheromones in the air!"

Holden adjusted the brim of his hat and reminded himself not to crack a smile. Mr. Snowden's eyes were twinkling up a storm, and he knew without a doubt that the old guy let his dog go onto her property a couple times a week simply for the entertainment of it—and for the offer of refreshments that always came afterward. And likely Mrs. Hutchinson's part in the whole affair was just as contrived.

As for Miss Bluebell, the huge gray cat was so old and fat that Holden had a feeling her refusal to exit the house was more about feline superiority and laziness than any pheromones that might be lingering in the air. He could see her even now, lounging in the golden light that bathed the pink pillow Mrs. Hutchinson kept for the cat in the bay window of her living room.

Holden hooked his thumbs into his belt loops and dutifully repeated the conversation he'd had with these two multiple times a week ever since accepting the job of sheriff on San Juan Island. "You don't have a fence, Mrs. Hutchinson. If you so adamantly want to keep Mr. Snowden's dog off your lawn, you really need to have one built."

The feisty woman used her cane to jab the box hedge that separated her property from Mr. Snowden's. "I do too have a fence."

Mr. Snowden folded his arms and leaned into his heels, all but grinning. The old guy knew the script of this conversation as well as Holden did.

"It's not a fence, Mrs. Hutchinson. It's got too many gaps to be considered a fence. The dog can easily slip through."

"He should keep it on a leash when it's outside!"

Holden shook his head. "He's not required to have the dog on a leash in his own yard, ma'am."

"But that mutt wasn't in *his* yard! It was in *my* yard, doing its best to water every plant on the premises!"

Holden looked at Mr. Snowden in expectation of his line.

"It is a *he*." The old man nodded definitively. "And *he's* got a name, same as your darn cat!"

Mrs. Hutchinson snorted. "Periwinkle isn't a name. It's a color."

"Oh, so you can name your cat Miss Bluebell"—Mr. Snowden flapped a hand at the cat—"but I can't name my dog Periwinkle?"

Said canine gave a woof at the sound of his master saying his name, drawing Holden's gaze to the scraggly looking shyster sitting on the walk in the patch of light spilling from Mr. Snowden's front door. The dog was indeed almost a bluish-purple color, which Holden could only assume had given rise to his name. He looked like he might be a cross between an Airedale and a Poodle and maybe something else that had long straight hair, because every tenth hair, or so, was about three inches longer than the curly ones around it and straight as a porcupine quill. Holden could quite honestly say he'd never seen an uglier mutt. And yet...

The dog, having noticed Holden's gaze on it, gave another yip and wagged his tail so hard that his entire backside wiggled as he sidled toward him.

Holden leaned across the hedge and patted the mutt's head. The dog was so ugly it couldn't help but be cute, if that made sense.

And now to bring this conversation to its conclusion. "Mr. Snowden, can you try to do better at keeping Periwinkle on your own side of the hedge?"

"Yes, sir, Sheriff Parker. I'll do my best, sir."

The dog was enjoying the pat on the head so much, that Holden leaned across with both hands to give him a really good rub.

"Traitor," Mrs. Hutchinson muttered. But there was a gleam of amusement in her eyes when she offered. "Since you're out at this time of night, I presume you have the night shift? Can I get you a cup of coffee, Sheriff? It's the least I could do for troubling you to come all this way."

"A cup of coffee sounds lovely, ma'am." He touched the brim of his hat.

The woman glanced across the hedge. "And I don't suppose it would be neighborly of me to ask the sheriff and not you. I've fresh lemon pound cake that came out of the oven only an hour ago. Would you care to join us, Henry?"

Henry Snowden almost kicked up his heels. "Don't mind if I do. I'll put Periwinkle in the house. Come on, boy." He snapped his fingers and hustled up his walk. A treat probably awaited Periwinkle inside for fulfilling his part of this little enactment. No doubt Henry had smelled the pound cake and launched a mission to get himself invited for a piece.

Holden shook his head with a grin as he followed Mrs. Hutchinson through her front door. "You get your room rented yet, ma'am?"

She sighed as she set about slicing generous portions of pound cake. "Not yet. Tilly Johnson thought her granddaughter might be moving back to the island, but it turned out she decided to move to Los Angeles instead. Imagine!" She made a clucking sound as though to say the girl was as good as lost to the world. "The only other applicants I've had were men, and you know how I feel about that."

Holden nodded. "Yes, ma'am. I'll keep my ear to the ground for you." He knew the elderly woman could use the supplement to her fixed income.

Henry knocked on the doorframe and poked his head inside, hat clutched to his chest.

Mrs. Hutchinson motioned him in, and when he settled at his usual spot at her kitchen table, she set the largest slice of cake before him and nudged a mug closer. "I made yours decaf and fixed it with two teaspoons of cream, the way you like it."

Holden couldn't help a grin as he pulled out his chair at the table.

Yes, indeed. The cases out here on the island might not be as adrenaline inducing as his last position, but he'd take lemon pound cake and faux squabbles with a smile and a light step.

This job was exactly what he needed after his years in Seattle.

The baked goods he got for his trouble were a nice bonus.

And at least out here, he'd never been responsible for the death of someone he was supposed to be protecting.

The cigarette snuffed out beneath the toe of Gandry Wright's black boot. A chill wind gusted down the Everett street from the west and slipped beneath the collar of his jacket. He zipped his coat tighter. The boss was not going to be happy about this latest development.

From the darkness of the garage, he studied the woman doing the CPR on Treyvon—or whatever his real name was. Would she bring him back to life? More importantly, did he have time to run out there and get that phone before the cops showed? But then she would see him and need to be dealt with. And a crowd was already forming—spilling out of the bank, the diner just across the way, the Mexican restaurant down the block.

Besides, he could already hear the first sirens—the police station was only a couple blocks from here. That was likely where Treyvon had been headed. Good thing they'd gotten to him first. He gave himself a little shake. It wouldn't do for the blue jackets to find him hiding in this garage. Hands thrust deep inside the pockets of his cargo pants, he strolled down the block to join the little group in front of the bank.

"What happened?" He directed his question to a little old lady with a Golden Retriever on a leash.

She shook her head and blew a sharp sound of disgust. "I didn't see. Probably gang related. Looks like that man might be dead!"

Gandry could only hope he would stay that way. As much as Treyvon knew, he could be a real detriment. Served the sneak right. Trying to infiltrate their group with his rank five-oh carcass. Too bad he'd sprinted before Gandry had a chance to pat him down. He hadn't expected the man to run when confronted with the fact that they knew he was a UC. But look at him now. Gandry hoped this would send a strong message to the rest of the pigs. Stay away. Come to think of it, how had the people on the inside let this one slip through their defenses?

Two cop cars screeched to a stop from opposite directions of the street at nearly the same moment. Four cops he didn't recognize spilled out and scanned the people gathered along the sidewalks, hands resting on their guns. Gandry wished he'd picked a spot farther to the back of the little crowd but didn't dare move now. That would draw too much attention. Thankfully, after a cursory glance, the blue jackets seemed more intent on helping the dark-haired woman and seeing to Treyvon.

Gandry withheld a smile, anxiously watching to see the moment one of them might recognize the scum who was one of their own.

One of the cops brushed the petite woman in the waitress uniform aside and took over the CPR.

As though her legs didn't have the strength to carry her farther, she sank to the pavement as another cop squatted beside her and spoke in tones too low for Gandry to make out above the murmur of the people near him.

The woman brushed dirt from her knees and plucked her phone from the pavement.

Gandry's stomach clenched. In the darkness, he hadn't seen what she'd done with Treyvon's phone. And it was obviously too late to get it now. How much information did Trey have on it?

Suddenly his biggest worry wasn't whether one of these officers might decide to question him.

He was going to have to come up with a mighty good explanation to keep the boss from offing him for this little mistake.

A mighty good explanation.

He raised his phone, zoomed in on the woman's face, and snapped a shot.

Detective Damien Packard stood outside Sheila Ellingsworth's Everett apartment. He swallowed and stared at the gold number eight on the red door. He chuckled and rolled his eyes at himself. He could face down hardened criminals, but paying a call on a beautiful woman had his stomach doing flips.

Pulling in a breath, he adjusted the bag of groceries and knocked.

He heard her touch the doorknob inside. There was a pause. And then the chain rattled and the door opened.

Sheila leaned her cheek against the door jam and smiled at him, her dark curls cascading over one shoulder. "You can't keep bringing me stuff."

It was good to see her smile. A memory flashed. Her, beaten and bloodied, cowering in the corner with her arms around her head while two officers cuffed her now ex-husband.

Damien blinked the memory away and offered the bag. "It's not much. How you doing?"

"Better now." She took the groceries and motioned for him to follow her inside. "Coffee?"

"Always."

"Brownies?"

He grinned. "Your favorites from that bakery—the ones with the cream cheese frosting—are in the bag."

She gave a little groan. "You know I've put on five pounds since you've been...coming around?"

He didn't miss that she hadn't quite known what to call their relationship—he wasn't sure he knew how to categorize it yet, either. He swept her with an appreciative look. "You could stand to put on more."

She spun to face him, eyes wide with humor, as she continued to back toward the kitchen. "Officer Packard! Don't you go speaking such negativity into my life!"

He shook his head and grabbed her arm to stop her because she was about to back into the counter. "Not negativity. Healthy. And you could never be anything but beautiful." He stroked his thumb across her skin, willing her to believe him.

She tucked her lower lip between her teeth and studied him for a long moment.

He let her look. Maybe this would be the moment she'd finally take this...friendship to the next phase. Her husband's abuse, both physical and mental, had damaged her in ways she was still healing from. Likely would always have to battle. All he wanted was a chance to battle alongside her.

As though some alarm inside her head had just clanged a warning, she tore her gaze from his and spun to the counter. "Well, you're kind for saying so. But a girl can't live on sweets alone." Despite her words, she was already pulling the plastic container of brownies from the bag. She waggled it and batted her lashes. "You do know the way to this girl's heart. Did you bring any of the chocolate chip cookies you like so much?" She peeked back into the bag.

He leaned against the island, resting his weight on folded arms as he smiled at her. "Nah. Only the brownies for you."

She planted her palms on the counter and leaned toward him. "You do know how to get past all my armor, Detective."

"What other weaknesses should I know about?"

Alarm flashed in her eyes and, too late, he realized he'd phrased that poorly.

She gave a forced chuckle and turned for the cupboard, but tension filled the line of her shoulders. "No one said anything about weakness."

"Sheila, I'm sor—"

"No. I'm sorry." She sighed and faced him from across the room. "You've never given me any reason to think you'd want to hold a weakness over me. I just—" She ran trembling hands over her face and forked her fingers into her hair. "You've been more than patient with me, Damien. I'm trying."

He remained where he was. "I'm not going anywhere, Sheil. I'm right here."

She nodded. Blinked a couple times. Then seemed to gather herself. She set two plates on the island and nudged the clamshell of brownies. "I could totally say no to these if I wanted to. Besides..." She glanced at him through her lashes as she popped open the lid and lifted two brownies onto the plates. "You have to let a girl keep some of her secrets."

Wow. He liked this girl a lot. It took grit for her to dial the conversation back to the mood he'd intended his comment to carry. "I'm a detective, you know. Ferreting out secrets is my job."

She smiled and was just handing him one of the plates when his cell phone rang. It was his partner, Case Lexington. He narrowed his eyes. This better be good. "Case, what's up?"

His partner's voice was full of tension when he said, "An officer has been murdered. That kid Treyvon Johnson. Remember him? We're up."

Damien sighed, heart plummeting. "On my way."

"On Hewitt. Between Colby and Hoyt."

He let his gaze linger on Sheila's features, tucking her beauty away to sustain him through what was sure to be a gut-wrenching night. "I'm thirty minutes out, if traffic is good."

"Maybe meet me at the precinct, then. I'm headed to the scene now to pick up a witness."

"Will do." Damien ended the call.

At least there was disappointment in Sheila's eyes. That was something else to tide him through.

He reached out and lifted the brownie from the plate she was still holding toward him. He raised it in a salute. "Can't stick around for the coffee, but I'll take this for the road."

She tilted her head. "Stay safe, hear?"

With one last lingering look, he backed reluctantly toward the door. "I'll do my best."

"Breakfast in the morning?"

He winced. "Have a feeling this one might be a long night. Doubt I'll be free by then."

She sighed and licked a bit of frosting from her thumb. "All right. I'll...see you when I see you then."

He gave her a hang-loose gesture and slipped into the night.

Man, sometimes he hated this job.

Chapter 3

Camryn pressed a trembling hand to her forehead. For a brief moment, she'd feared that the driver of the coupe had returned to finish her off. To her relief, it had been the police arriving. But her heart was still hammering like a rock-band drummer.

She would like nothing better than to wake up and realize this was all a terrible nightmare. But the broken voice of the officer pronouncing the victim's death rang with a note of undeniable authenticity that imprisoned her in the real world. A world that was grimmer than any nightmare she'd had in a very long time. One that sent a chill straight through her. As did the rough asphalt of the Everett street beneath her.

She looked to where a couple officers draped a white covering over the victim. His hand—the one she'd gripped only moments ago—had flopped out to the side far enough that the sheet draped across the back of it. A stark contrast against his dark skin, even in this dim lighting.

Grief moistened her eyes. Odd that she should grieve for a man she'd never known. Yet, his life had been in her hands and she'd failed to save him.

An officer squatted next to her. "Sorry to disturb you, ma'am. Thank you for trying to save him. Are you the witness?"

Camryn scanned the crowds gathering on both sides of the street. Where had everyone appeared from? Was she the only witness to the hit-and-run out of all these people? Surely not. Yet she didn't remember seeing anyone else on the sidewalks as she'd walked toward the bus stop from the diner. It was dark, yes, but the streetlights had revealed no one.

How sad for the man that she'd been the only witness of the violence that led to his death. Did he have a family? Wife? Kids?

"Ma'am?" the officer prodded.

Camryn shifted. "Yes. I think I was the only one to see...it."

"I'm Officer Skelly. I'm going to have to ask you to come down to the station and give a statement."

She swallowed. She had an early shift tomorrow. This was going to make it a short night. But what else could she do? She nodded. "What's going to happen to him?"

Officer Skelly stood, then stretched down a hand to help her to her feet. "The police aren't allowed to touch the body now that he's been pronounced. The ME will take care of him. But they can't get in here until the detectives and CSI have processed the scene."

"So, he's just going to lie there?"

The man glanced toward the body with a grim set to his jaw as he indicated with a gesture that she should precede him to one of the patrol cars. "We will get the scene processed as quickly as we can. But trust me. We all want to get Tr—him off the street as soon as possible."

There was something about his tone that made her look up at him. "You knew him?"

He opened the back door of the black and white for her. "He was one of us, ma'am. Undercover."

She'd witnessed the murder of an undercover police officer? The thought took the strength from her legs. She sank into the patrol car.

It wasn't until Officer Skelly started to shut the door that she remembered the phone. "Wait." She tugged the device from her apron pocket. "He...he asked me to give this to... Does 'pack police' mean anything to you?"

Officer Skelly's brow furrowed. "Pack police?"

Camryn worried her teeth over her lower lip searching her memory of the victim's words. "I think that's what he said. I know he said the word 'police.'"

"You did the right thing. I'll ask some of the others to see if that means anything to them." He took a set of gloves from a pocket of his vest, tugged them on, then took the device, gingerly gripping only the edges.

She immediately realized he was trying not to smear any fingerprints. She hadn't even thought about that. "I'm sorry. I should have handled it more carefully."

He gave her a gentle smile that said she shouldn't worry as he slipped the phone into a plastic bag, sealed it, then marked something on the outside with a black felt pen. "I'll just let my—"

Down the street, through one of the police cars' bullhorns, an officer's voice bellowed instructions for everyone in the crowd to please stay on the sidewalks. It prevented Camryn from hearing the end of Officer Skelly's sentence, but she gathered by the way he held up one finger before he walked away that she should wait.

She closed the door and tilted her head against the back of the seat, eyes closed.

There was no way she could fall asleep with all this adrenaline pumping through her, and yet her body buzzed with an exhaustion that left her feeling in limbo somewhere between collapse and hysteria.

Pack police... What could it mean?

Officer Laurence Miller arrived at the scene and took in the chaos. He climbed from his car and stopped next to the body, scanning the crowd. Where was Gandry? He had to be here. How could he have made such a critical error? This could mean the end of their whole operation. The body was supposed to be disposed of in a way that brought no attention to it. He cursed under his breath. This was going to draw a lot of scrutiny.

His phone buzzed in his pocket. He tugged it out. His lips pressed together.

There was a zoomed-in pixelated image of a woman. Followed by, *she's got his phone.*

With a sigh he deleted the message and thrust the phone back into his pocket.

Once more, it fell to him to clean up someone else's mess.

Ryan Skelly maintained his professional demeanor, but inside he felt the familiar jitters that came with any big break in a case.

He scanned the melee of officers surrounding the victim, searching for Captain Danielson. If Treyvon had felt his phone important enough to trust it to a stranger with instructions to get it to the police, surely it had something on it that they could use to discover who had killed him.

Skelly hadn't been with the Everett force long, and some of the guys still made it clear they felt he was an outsider. This might be just the thing he needed to prove he was one of them.

"Skelly, what you got there?" Officer Laurence Miller spoke from behind him.

He turned. Maybe Miller would know where the captain was. He held up the bag with the phone in it. "Treyvon gave this to the witness."

Miller's brows rose. "To the woman who did CPR on him? Did he say anything to her?"

Skelly shook his head. "She only said he told her something like 'pack police.' She wasn't sure she got it right. That mean anything to you?"

"Pack police..." Miller mulled over the words as he took the evidence bag and examined the smashed phone, front and back. "Can't say that it does. I'll put this in my squad's evidence locker."

Skelly snatched it back before Miller could even take a step. At the surprised look on Miller's face, he shrugged. "She entrusted it to me. I'll ask the captain. You seen him?"

"Last I saw, he was going to get something from his squad car. He's parked over there." Miller gestured to the SUV with flashing lights that blocked the alley between the parking garage and the bank. The car's headlights were strategically pointed to flood the middle of the street while still blocking the entrance.

"Great. I'll take this to him. It's important and he needs to see it right away. I'll be right back to help with interviews."

"Sounds good. Hey, where is this woman anyhow?"

Skelly gestured. "I sat her in the back of Sanderson's unit. It was the closest. Figured it was best to get her off the street as soon as possible."

Miller nodded. Gave him a thumbs up. "Good."

There it was again. The implication that because he was from Kansas, he might not understand the dangers of leaving a witness exposed in the middle of a street.

He gritted his teeth as he made his way to the back of Captain Danielson's cruiser. He wasn't sure what it was about Miller, but the man made his skin crawl.

The alley was dark and the strobing lights didn't do much to penetrate it. He reached the back of the vehicle and checked the far side without finding the captain. He paused to consider. Strange. Looked like he'd have to talk to him later. For now... He glanced down at the phone. An officer had died trying to get whatever was on this to the cops.

Smashed as it was, the phone likely wouldn't even power on. But he'd worked in data recovery for his department back in Wichita. It would speed the investigation along if they didn't have to wait for tech to get their hands on this device.

Decision made, he strode to his own car and slipped behind the wheel. It only took him seconds to power on his dashboard laptop. The software he needed was already installed. He snagged a pair of touchscreen gloves and a cord from his glovebox. He plugged the phone into the laptop. A few clicks later, data was dumping from the phone into his computer. The whole process took less than five minutes. He was unplugging the phone when the call came over the radio. "Skelly, Miller says you have the phone?"

That was the captain's voice.

He keyed his mic. "Yes sir. Locking it in my evidence boot." He didn't feel comfortable announcing over the air that he'd dumped the data from it too. He would tell the captain later. There were too many frequency surfers. Who knew who might be listening?

"I want to get that to tech, ASAP. I'm going back to the station now. Bring it."

Skelly resisted a roll of his eyes. Where had the man been a few minutes ago? "On my way, sir." At least now he could tell him that he'd dumped the data and it should be on the station servers.

He slipped out of the driver's seat and pivoted to retrace his steps. The captain's vehicle hadn't moved. But he still wasn't there. Skelly bent to get a closer look into the vehicle's interior.

The sound behind him barely registered before pain bloomed across the back of his skull and the world faded to black.

It was a bold move, slipping into another officer's cruiser in plain view of anyone paying attention. But with the darkness and all the flashing lights, Miller knew that if anyone happened to notice, they would simply think he was Skelly. If the man hadn't snatched that phone back out of his grasp a moment ago, none of this would have been necessary.

The driver's seat was still warm from Skelly sitting in it. He'd been watching. And he'd definitely seen Skelly's vehicle computer power up.

He didn't take time to see if he'd actually dumped the data from the phone. It didn't really matter now. What was done, was done.

It only took a few swift keystrokes of his gloved fingers to delete the hard-drive on the computer.

He exited the vehicle and casually walked toward a group of bystanders as he pulled his phone from his pocket. He shot off a text.

Done.

The reply came immediately. *Good. Taking care of it.*

He felt a measure of satisfaction as he stuffed the phone back into his pocket and scanned the crowd. He leveled them with a look that spanned the gap between friendly and approachable, and all-business. "Good evening, everyone. Who can tell me what they saw tonight?"

At a desk in the corner of the Everett Police Station, a hunched figure sat in deep concentration, fingers flying over the keyboard. Too bad about Officer Skelly. He'd been a good kid. Knew his stuff. If only he hadn't decided to dump that phone, they would have left him alone.

There it was! The file that had streamed into the police server at precisely 10:27 pm. A couple keystrokes zapped it into oblivion and he released a whoosh of breath as he sank against his seat.

For a brief moment he pondered the years when he'd kept his nose clean with a touch of nostalgia. Those had been the days. Back when his idealism with this job had still been bright and shiny. Before he realized that no matter how long and hard he fought, he would never be able to change the world. Never be able to get rid of all the crooks. Before he'd decided that if he was going to have any sort of retirement cushion, he needed to take matters into his own hands.

This Treyvon kid had nearly cost them. Imagine if he'd worked this long only to lose his pension? Well, he smirked, there was the nice cushion he'd built for himself over the last few years, but it was the pride of the thing. He wanted to still be able to attend functions with his buddies, and if this had gotten out, that definitely wouldn't have been an option.

He realized his hands were trembling and scooped them back through his hair. Well, no matter. Together they'd taken care of it.

But this had been close. Too close.

Camryn had only been in the car alone for a few minutes when a different officer slipped into the front seat. He glanced back through the wire mesh that separated them, and gave her a nod. "Evening, ma'am. I'm going to run you to the station now."

"Where's Officer Skelly?"

He waved a hand, then started the car. "He'll be tied up here for several hours yet."

Yes. She supposed he would. Perhaps the words Skelly had said a moment ago were that she should wait until another officer came to drive her to the station. That must have been it.

The man eased the nose of the car past a couple officers.

A man in a suitcoat and tie dashed up and banged on the hood with the flat of his palm. "Stop!"

A jolt zipped through Camryn's chest.

"Miller, stop! I've got this!"

The officer in the front seat rolled his eyes and his window whirred down. "I'm just running her to the station. Skelly said to."

"No. No."

Camryn couldn't see anything of the man protesting, other than that he reached for her door handle.

"Packard and I drew this case. She's my witness and I don't want anyone talking to her before we do." He wrenched open her door. "Ma'am, if you'd come with me please?"

The officer in the front seat met her eyes in the rearview mirror and there was suddenly a coldness about them that sent a chill down her spine. She pressed into the seat and debated her options. Maybe she should go home. The cops could call her and interview her later.

But the man outside her door bent and looked in at her, and there was something calming about his expression. "My car is right this way." He tipped a nod down the street and offered a hand to help her out.

And before she could change her mind, she fled the cold eyes glaring at her in the mirror.

Chapter 3

The detective helped her into his back seat, then climbed in front. He put his car into gear and eased away from the officer named Miller who had stepped from the other vehicle and now studied her through the back window of the car with cold eyes.

Camryn clutched her coat at her throat.

She studied her new driver—captor?—through the mesh grill of the car. Though the interior of the car was dark, she could tell he had blond hair, and when he met her glance for a brief moment in the rearview mirror his gaze was frank and open. He did have nice eyes, and a kind look. "Don't worry," he said. "You're safe with me."

But wasn't that what any man might say whether she was safe or not? Still, at least his frank expression gave her more reassurance than the last officer's had.

In the mirror, his gaze dipped to where she still clutched at the neck of her coat. "I'm taking you to the police station." He turned left at the next stop sign. "See? That's the building right up there." He pointed with his left hand and she caught the flash of a wedding band on his ring finger.

Why did that ease her tension? It eased a little more when he did pull into the parking garage beneath the station. "Why didn't you want that other man to bring me here?"

His gaze bounced off hers in the mirror before returning to concentrate on parking in a space right next to the elevators. "We just have a few questions for you."

An answer that wasn't really an answer at all. As he opened her door, she decided not to push. For the moment, she was content to not feel threatened.

The elevator doors whooshed open and it only took a few seconds to climb to the seventh floor.

At the door that led into the main precinct, the plain-clothed officer motioned for her to wait. He poked his head inside and checked both directions. Seemingly satisfied, he gestured for her to follow him. "Right this way." He quickly escorted her into an office with 'Deputy Chief' on the door plaque. They stepped past a messy desk and then through a side door into a drab room not much larger than the tiny bathroom in her apartment. Gray walls met gray ceiling, and the chipped stick-on linoleum tiles on the floor did nothing to help the room's appeal. Nor did the yellow leather couch that looked like it could have been transported here straight from the 1970s. A steel table surrounded by three plastic chairs was the only other item of note in the room.

"Please stay in here until we come for you." He started to shut the door.

"Wait! Please. I have to work an early shift. How long is this going to take?"

"We'll be with you shortly," the man clipped. And then he left, shutting the door to the office behind him.

Camryn sank onto the couch and rested her head into her hands. It was surprisingly more comfortable than she'd expected. A headache pinched. She massaged her temples, wishing for a cup of coffee. Maybe she'd just rest her head on the arm of the couch for a few minutes.

Gandry Wright braced his feet wide, fighting to maintain his balance on the tiny fishing boat. He paused his work and cast his gaze across the undulating water lit only by the milky spill of a full moon. Puget Sound always looked so calm from the shore. He never would have suspected that the gently rolling swells were actually more like rolling mountains intercut with steep troughs. When the boat bobbed to the top of a swell, he could see the golden glow of Everett's lights along the shore.

To the south, the sweeping strobe from the Mukilteo lighthouse sliced through the darkness, then his boat slid down the other side of the wave.

He shook his head. He didn't like being out here on the water all alone, but the boss had insisted this was the best way to get rid of the body. No matter. He would soon be done with the task and could head back to shore.

His hands cramped as he pried the last tooth from the dead man's skull and dropped it into the cold depths of the Sound. He would take care of the hands next. He worked his fingers in and out, before he reached for the saw and placed it against the skin of the man's wrist. It took a moment for the blade to catch and then it grated a sound that set his teeth on edge. He lurched for the side of the boat and for the first time that night, as he cast up the contents of his stomach, was glad to be the only one alive on this boat. He had a reputation for being the one to call to get anything done, but the truth was, he'd never been called on to cut up and dispose of a body before. Especially not the body of a freshly-murdered police officer.

Allowing himself two deep inhales he put the saw back to work. "Sorry man. No one deserves to go out this way. But..." he shrugged one shoulder. "I know you understand that I'm only doing what I have to. I don't want to end up like you, if you catch my drift."

The strategically placed five-gallon bucket that he'd purchased at the big box store specifically for this job caught the severed hand when it fell.

He ought to toss the parts as he cut them, but he felt a little squeamish still. The thought of that severed hand laying in the bottom of the bucket made his stomach roil. Crazy since he'd just sawed the thing off. He would toss everything one by one once the whole of this was done. Then he'd go home and drink until he couldn't hold another shot.

He moved the bucket, first beneath the other hand, then the head, then one of the feet.

He had just started in on the last foot when he heard it.

He froze and jerked his head up. His little boat swooped through the valley of one trough and started up the other side of a swell. The sound swept in again. The mosquito drone of another boat engine.

Panic crashed through him, sending his pulse into overdrive.

Music accompanied the engine noise and above it all, whoops of laughter. From the top of the swell, he could see the brightly lit deck of a small pleasure-craft. Whoever was on the boat obviously wasn't trying to hide out here in the darkness. And they were bearing right down on him!

His boat sank into the sound-proofing swells of water.

Wide-eyed, he surveyed his tiny boat. The headless, handless, corpse lay draped across the benches. Blood was everywhere. And he had a saw in his hands! Any people that got close, couldn't miss the details in the wash of this blasted full moon. And how much more so if the brightness of those party lights turned his way!

Though the corpse still had one foot halfway attached, and the uniform still on, he didn't have time to complete the job. He would simply have to hope that the body didn't wash ashore before the foot and clothes were devoured by fish and sea.

He chucked the saw into the waves and scrabbled to maintain his balance as another wave rocked his boat to the top of a crest.

"Yo! There's a boat!" He heard a young male voice yell, before he once more sank out of sight.

He heaved the body over the side. Something clunked against the bucket but a thought seized him. Was the body going to float? He hesitated, breaths beating against his teeth. He couldn't have been more relieved when it disappeared into the black waters without so much as even a burble. He snatched up the lid of the bucket and used it to sluice sheets of water over the boat, not caring that he was also soaking himself in the process.

Good enough, now he only had to get rid of the parts. He reached for the bucket. He would just toss—

"Yo! Whatcha doin' out here this time o' night?" A drunken voice called. "Don'tcha know it's dangerous?" Hoots of laughter followed.

Gandry slammed the lid onto the five-gallon bucket and slung it over the side. It splashed into the water behind him as he lifted a friendly wave to the occupants of the other vessel. He thumbed a gesture over his shoulder. "Just dropping my crab pots!"

One of the boys pointed back in the direction they'd arrived from. "Ferry just left. You better clear this lane."

"Yep!" Gandry waved. "I'm leaving now." He started his engine and pulled away. He cursed under his breath. He certainly hoped the boss wasn't going to ask him to do too many more jobs like that one.

Stress like that could take a few years off a man's life.

In the dark cold waters of the Sound, the five-gallon bucket bobbed and swayed.

On the boat, the two boys looked at each other. "Doesn't he know this is a stupid place to crab? The ferries will destroy his pots."

The other boy shrugged and stepped behind the wheel. "Must be a newb." He pushed the engine into gear. "Best get home or my dad won't let me use the boat for our party this weekend."

"Can't have that," the other boy said. "You man the helm. I'm going to trawl awhile."

"You already caught your limit!"

"So! We ate 'em." With surprising skill, considering his state of drunkenness, he flipped the net in a wide arc behind the boat. "Who'll know if we catch more?"

Their laughter covered the clunk of the bucket's handle rapping against itself as it snagged in the net.

An hour later, drowsy from the effects of their inebriation, the boys swept into Friday Harbor.

"Whoa! Whoa! You're gonna hit the dock!" One of them lurched for the controls and yanked the engine into reverse.

A backwash of water surged through the net, knocking one lucky fish and the bucket free.

"Idiot!" the boy slapped the driver on the back of his head.

"Sorry, man! I'm tired!"

The other boy chuckled. "How can you be tired? It's freezing out here!"

A curse slipped free as the kid stepped from the wheel house. "You're right. It was warm in there." His thumb jabbed over his shoulder.

His friend nudged him toward the dock. "Go home and sleep it off. I'll bring by your half of the fish in the morning. Your dad will be happy with the catch."

In the shoals, the tide swirled the bucket into the current that curled around the northern promontory. It bobbed for several hundred feet along the shore, and then caught fast on a reef of coral as the tide swept out.

In a pine tree, an owl hooted a lonely cry into the night.

Chapter 4

Holden Parker felt the icy slicing wind blowing off the Salish Sea in the very marrow of his bones as he squatted on the edge of a San Juan Island promontory and studied the bright orange bucket swishing in the low-tide surf below.

Dawn had barely spread a pink tinge on the water.

Since he'd worked the swing shift tonight, he'd barely crawled into his bed when this call had dragged him out again. And he hadn't even taken time to brew a cup of coffee.

In disgust, he tossed down the long branch he'd been using to try to snag the bucket closer. The water wasn't deep here and the rocks were preventing the just-out-of-reach bucket from coming closer.

"Did Mr. Hendrix say when he spotted it?" he asked his deputy, Jay Powers.

Jay, squatting next to him, shook his head. "He only said that he was here fishing yesterday and it wasn't here. So, it washed in with the tide sometime during the night. He said it was clanking against the rocks and he hadn't had a bite all morning."

Holden glanced up to see the subject of their conversation giving a hearty wave from his schooner a quarter mile from the shore.

"Emergency my left foot." Holden grumbled as he assessed the situation. He didn't want to get wet. He really didn't. But the bucket was too near to shore for a boat, and they'd tried every tool they had that might work. The handle on their net was too short, besides which, the bucket might be too heavy to lift from this distance and the rocks here were sharp and might cut the net if they dragged it.

There was also the consideration that if the bucket held something sinister, they really ought to record the area around it in case it was needed as evidence. They could go back to the office for the department's dinghy, or for the waders, but that seemed like a lot of work for such a silly thing.

He glanced over at his deputy.

Jay winced and sighed.

But Holden waved him off. "Seem to recall that you were the one who got down in that sewer ditch when Mrs. Sorenson's cat got stuck in that pipe last month."

Jay looked hopeful. "I was."

"Besides, I need something to wake me up." Holden reached to unlace his boots. If he had to get wet, at least he wanted dry socks and shoes to put back on afterwards. He balanced awkwardly on first one foot, then the other to remove his socks without getting them wet, then stuffed the socks into the tops of the boots. He rolled his pants up to his knees, then slipped on a pair of evidence gloves.

The bucket wasn't out far, but this was still going to be torture.

He couldn't withhold a gasp as he stepped down into the lapping icy water. "Dang!" It was the worst his language ever got, but even that word didn't seem to cut muster in this instance. At least he was no longer feeling drowsy.

Though yesterday had been nearly sixty degrees, temperatures had plummeted overnight and ice had formed along the edge of the shore. Cold didn't begin to describe the water. His toes spasmed and cramped and already he could barely feel them. He'd be lucky if he didn't come out of this with a smashed toe.

He hurried as quickly as he could through the rocky shoals. He didn't want to lose his balance and end up wet from head to toe. It didn't take him more than a few seconds to get to the lidded bucket, but he couldn't just snatch it and run back to the shore. He clamped his teeth together to keep them from chattering as he used his phone to snap a series of pictures of the bucket's position and the water all around it.

By the time he got back to the bank and handed it up, his feet were so numb that Jay had to help him out of the water. The towel Jay tossed to him, actually felt warm, even though it had been in the utility box in the back of their truck and it was thirty-three degrees outside.

Holden sank onto a rock and tugged his socks and boots on as quickly as possible.

"Do we open it here?" Jay asked.

Holden shook his head. There was too much risk of whatever was in the bucket getting contaminated if they opened it out here. Not that it was likely to be anything important. "Let's get this back to the station, then we can crack it open and see what we've found."

There was another bonus about opening the bucket back at headquarters. He wouldn't say anything, but he hoped that Jay would crank the heat on the way back to the station.

And bless the man's heart, he did just that as they pulled away from the shore, leaving Mr. Hendrix waving behind them. "Want to take bets on what's in it?" Jay grinned. "I'm betting it's...firecrackers that floated away from some shoreline home a few months ago."

Holden flipped the dial on their old truck's heating vents to direct the heat to his still-aching feet. "Likely as good a guess as any. Maybe it's full of treasure that has been languishing at the bottom of the ocean for three hundred years and bobbed to the surface only last night."

Jay rolled his eyes. "Yeah, because five-gallon buckets have obviously been around that long."

Holden waved a hand. "There goes my theory, I guess." He huddled into his coat, trying not to look as miserable as he felt. At least some of the feeling was returning to his feet now.

By the time they pulled into the parking lot at the station, he was starting to feel human again.

Kate Dollinger looked up from the reception desk, salt-and-pepper brows peaking as Holden followed Jay who carried the bucket through the door. "What have we here?"

Holden ignored her.

Jay only offered, "Bucket."

Holden bit back a grin. Seemed Jay was as tired of Kate's curiosity as he was.

Truth was, if he had any other person on the island that he felt he could talk into doing the job, he'd let Kate go in a heartbeat. She was much too nosy for the position. And too many times he'd caught wind of people knowing information they could only have learned from Kate. The job of receptionist at a police station required someone incurious and unflappable, and Kate lacked both qualities.

She rose from her desk and followed them across the room. "Oh my. Where did you find that? What's in it?"

They stepped into the side room that normally functioned as the station's interrogation room. But in this case the table would be used to examine the evidence.

The small room barely had space for the table and four chairs. Other than those, the one overhead light, and the two-way window, the room contained nothing else.

Jay was already stacking the four chairs in the far corner.

Holden nudged Kate out of the room. "You'll know anything we need you to know when the time comes."

"But—"

He shut the door. And then gave the blinds a twist, because even though he couldn't see her from this side of the window, he knew she, at this very moment, had her face pressed up against the glass.

With nothing between them and the orange bucket on the table now, the two men stood over it as they donned rubber gloves.

Jay asked, "Ready?"

Holden nodded and gripped the base of the bucket. "Go ahead." Island life must really be boring him if a little curiosity over a bucket could get his pulse skipping a few beats. His lips twisted in a smirk.

The plastic of the lid was new and stiff. It creaked and resisted. Jay worked his way around it, prying it up a little at a time. It hinged toward Holden, blocking his view. Jay glanced inside. "Dear God!" He leapt back so quickly that the lid clattered from his hand and rolled into the corner.

Holden's brows shot up. He leaned forward and looked into the bucket. His heart stilled. What had he just been thinking about island life not being exciting enough? His stomach curled. This was worse than anything he'd ever seen while working homicide.

Inside the bucket lay a severed head, a foot, and maybe a few other parts beneath. The lid must not have been sealed all the way because the bucket was half filled with murky water that had swollen the tissues till they were almost unrecognizable for what they were.

He glanced at Jay who was still trying to gather himself in the corner. A case like this would stick with the kid for a while. Holden adjusted the bands of his rubber gloves and lifted the upper lip of the dead man. His teeth had all been pulled out. "A few more hours in the water and this poor guy would have been unidentifiable."

With one hand propped against the wall in the corner of the room, Jay scrubbed a wrist over his forehead and spoke over his shoulder. "Think we'll be able to get prints to identify him?"

"Probably." Holden glanced back into the bucket. Something metallic caught his eye. He nudged aside the foot. His heart sank. The metallic object in the bottom of the bucket was a police badge. "But we won't have to wait that long."

The call came into the Everett Police Station just after five o'clock.

Detective Damien Packard could hardly believe the news. Ryan Skelly was a newer transfer to their department. He hadn't worked here long, but Damien liked him. He couldn't fathom that he was gone. Much less in such a manner.

It was bad enough that Treyvon Johnson had been killed. But now Skelly too?

Worse yet, this news confirmed what he and Case had been afraid of for several months now. There was a dirty cop in their precinct—maybe more than one.

He hadn't known Treyvon all that well. The kid was barely past his training and had been undercover for most of the time since he'd been approved. But his first day as a rookie, his T.O. had been out sick and Damien had been assigned to the kid. They'd only spent that one day together, but Damien had liked the kid. He was made of the right stuff for this job. His death was beyond a tragedy.

And now to find out this...

Sheriff Holden Parker, the officer Case had worked with last year on a drug bust, was on his way here via chopper with what was most likely Skelly's partial remains. Skelly, who'd been investigating Treyvon's death just the night before. What had happened to Skelly last night? One minute, officers said he'd been at the scene and then he'd simply seemed to vanish.

Lexington strode toward him. His face was grim. "We really need to interview that witness. She's been in the interrogation room off the deputy chief's office all night. He's not on the roster today, so I figured that was the best place to put her."

"Right." Damien stood wearily. "Now's as good a time as any."

Lexington strode toward the break room. "I'll get coffee."

Before Case had taken two steps, Captain Danielson poked his head out of his office. "Lexington! Packard! My office!" He disappeared again without giving them a chance to reply.

When they arrived in his office, it was to find Laurence Miller and his partner, Jack Kingston, already present. Captain Danielson was behind his desk, but not sitting. Arms folded, he leaned into his heels and glowered at them. "Miller tells me you snatched the witness from the scene last night?"

Damien clasped his hands behind his back in an at-attention pose, seeing Case do the same from the corner of his eye. Damien kept his mouth shut, letting Case formulate the reasoning behind his actions.

"We drew this one, Captain."

Captain Danielson's palm slapped down on his desk with so much force that a pencil jumped and rolled off. "I know you drew the case! But Miller says you dressed him down in front of a whole crowd of people!"

"No, sir. That's not the way I saw it, sir."

"How *did* you see it?"

"She was our witness, sir. We drew the... But you already know that."

The captain leaned across his desk, eyes spitting fire. He brought his face to within inches of Case's. "Are you yanking my chain, Lexington?"

Damien clamped his teeth to keep from coming to Case's defense. It wouldn't do his partner any good. Nor would mentioning that he hadn't been at the scene of the hit-and-run because he'd been taking a bag of groceries to the ex-wife of an abuser they'd arrested last year. The captain wouldn't care that the broken woman had captivated his heart and kindled his every protective instinct. Ever since the captain's wife had come down with cancer several months back, he'd been surly and irritable. The whole precinct had been walking on eggshells for weeks now.

"No, sir. I'm not yanking your chain, sir." Case was at full attention.

The captain seemed satisfied with that, because he eased back a little. "Very well. Where is she?"

Damien heard Case swallow. They couldn't reveal that they had her in a concealed interrogation room because they didn't trust their fellow officers. Not until they had proof, at any rate. But the very fact that Miller and Kingston had toddled in here to tattle on them, bumped them up several notches on the suspect list.

Case still hadn't replied and the silence was stretching too long. Captain Danielson's eyebrow twitched.

"We were just about to interview her, sir." Damien was careful not to fidget under the captain's gaze. "We wanted to be the first to speak to her so that we would have unmuddied testimony. But we'll be happy to make her available to speak to others as soon as we've concluded our interview."

"You'll be happy to—" The captain's voice trailed off, his tone revealing his astonished irritation.

It was time to send the punch all the way through. "Have you ever been displeased with any of our investigations, Captain? Lexington's and mine?" He gave a beat for the captain to ponder before hurrying ahead. "I'd venture to say the answer to that is a firm no. Because we produce results. And we are able to do that because we are very particular about the way we do things—including how we interview eye-wit—"

All their radios blared at the same time. "All units, SCJ is reporting an escape. I need several units to move that way. Missing from roll call is Vossler. Kirk Vossler. Six foot, brown hair, brown eyes, medium build."

"What the—" Captain Danielson was already racing for his door. "Miller. Kingston. You're with me! We'll finish this discussion later."

Case and Damien were left in the captain's office, staring at one another. An escapee at the Snohomish County Jail?

Case's brow furrowed. "Wasn't he the guy who was convicted of inciting that riot?"

"Pretty sure. Yeah."

"Let's hope it's a false alarm." Case batted his arm with the back of his hand. "Doesn't matter to us right now. Let's get this interview done and try to get this witness out of here before

Miller and Kingston get back. My alarm bells go off every time either of them are in the room."

Damien sighed and followed Case back into the main part of the office. He knew exactly what Case meant. There were too many little coincidences surrounding that team. Miller in particular. But they had no proof.

For now, their biggest priority had to be the safety of this witness. With two people involved in last night's incident already turning up dead, they couldn't take any chances with her life.

Chapter 5

Camryn couldn't have said exactly how much time had passed when she woke. She lurched upright, and for a moment confusion had her searching the room as she tried to figure out where she was. The memories rushed in with a jolting clarity and she realized she'd fallen asleep.

What time was it? She tugged her phone from her apron. Nearly five! Panic swirled through her. She had to be to work in three hours. She'd slept here all night? No wonder she had a kink in her neck. She reached to massage it.

Maybe now was the time to set aside her qualms about God. She closed her eyes. "Lord, I know it's been awhile. But if ever I needed you to show up, it's now. You know how tight my finances are. I need to get to work. I can't jeopardize this job! So if you could please speed this along and get me out of here, I'd appreciate it." She felt a little guilty at the selfishness of the prayer in the wake of what she'd witnessed the night before, so tacked on a quick request that the people responsible would be caught.

The door from the deputy chief's office opened, jolting her out of her prayer. Either this was the quickest answer to prayer in the history of the universe, or God had a cruel sense of humor.

A grim-faced man plopped a file folder on the table and sank into one of the seats. A different man than the one who'd brought her here. But about the same age, she guessed. Late twenties? Early thirties? His rawboned face sported a couple days' worth of scruff.

"Sorry it took so long for us to get to you," he said. "I'm Detective Damien Packard. My partner is the one who brought you here." The detectives were younger than she might have expected men of their profession to be.

Camryn stood from the couch and took the lone seat on her side of the table. She glanced at her blurry reflection in the tabletop. It distorted even further as memories of the accident formed a horror film that kept replaying in her mind.

She lifted her gaze to the man across from her.

He silently returned her scrutiny.

He looked bone weary. His hair was dark, and he had striking light brown eyes and a hard set to his jaw that made her pity any criminal who crossed his path. But when he spoke, his voice was not unkind. "I'm sorry for all you've been through tonight."

Camryn rubbed at a mark on the steel tabletop. "I only wish I could have helped—" Her voice broke and she cleared her throat.

The man folded his hands and leaned forward, casual but attentive. "I listened to the tape of your 911 call. Sounds like you did all you could. My partner will be here soon and—"

"I'm here." Behind him, the blond man who'd brought her to the station pushed the door open with his hip, balancing three cups with a stack of napkins on top. "I figured we could all use some coffee." He set the three lidded Styrofoam cups on the table and then stretched his hand to her. "I'm Detective Case Lexington, Detective Packard's partner. Sorry we didn't get a proper introduction earlier. I was in a bit of a hurry."

She took his hand. "Camryn Hunt."

He set the napkins aside and nudged one of the cups in her direction. "Cream? Sugar?" He pulled some packets and stir sticks from his shirt pocket and tossed them all on the table.

The coffee smelled divine. "This is fine. Thank you. When will I be able to leave?"

Neither of the men answered her. Detective Packard was the one who spoke. "We'd like you to tell us everything you saw last night, Camryn. Try not to leave out anything. We'll prod for details if we need to clarify. But the most important thing you need to realize is that you're not in any trouble here. We appreciate how cooperative you are being." He placed his phone in the middle of the table. "We do need to record this conversation so we can refer back to it later. Is that all right with you?"

"Yes. That's fine," Camryn said.

Detective Lexington gave her an encouraging smile. "Just start at the beginning."

Camryn took a fortifying sip of coffee and then told them how she'd left work and been on her way to the bus stop. Once she started to speak, the words seemed to gush out of her and the detectives listened closely, jotting notes once in a while. They held their silence until she got to the end.

"…then you drove me here." She studied the detective, still wondering about the way he'd commandeered the situation with the other officer who'd been about to drive her away from the scene of the…she couldn't quite bring herself to call it an accident. "Why did you step in and insist on driving me back here yourself?"

Detective Packard looked up from consulting his notes. "You're certain you were alone on the street?"

Camryn didn't miss that he hadn't given his partner time to answer, but she decided to let it pass. She considered. "I didn't see anyone, but…"

"Yes?"

"In the garage. I saw an orange glow. Like someone might have been smoking a cigarette. They might have seen something."

Detective Lexington jotted some notes.

Detective Packard gave her a nod. "We'll check that out. Now, let's talk about the car. What color was it?"

She shook her head. "It was dark. The headlights were pointing right at me for most of the time it was in view. I'm not sure I can say for sure."

His lips pressed together. "Are there any other details you can give us?"

Camryn closed her eyes. She didn't want to revisit the memories yet again, but she forced herself to focus on what she'd seen. The car skidding around the corner. Headlights blinding her. The crash. The pause. A tremor zipped through her as she once more saw the car bearing down on her and then at the last moment turning away.

"Gray?" She pressed her hands together and opened her eyes. "I think the car was dark gray or dark blue. I'm not good with types of cars, but it was an older car. One of those kinds that is wider at the front end than the back. And it was raised up...like, taller than a normal car. Maybe a little higher in the front than the back." Another memory surfaced. "And I think it has a taillight out. When it drove away, it only had one red light at the back."

Detective Packard nodded encouragingly. "All this is very helpful." He consulted his notes. "You said you gave the man's phone to an officer. But you didn't say his name. Do you know who it was?"

"He said his name was Officer Skelly."

The two detectives looked at each other.

This time it was Detective Lexington who spoke. "When was the last time you saw Officer Skelly?"

"He escorted me to the car. I gave him the phone. A few minutes later a different officer—I never got his name, but the one you took over from—got in the car and said he was going to bring me here. You know the rest." She recalled the man's cold eyes staring at her in the rearview mirror and shivered. "He wasn't going to bring me here, was he?"

"Did Officer Skelly say anything to you? After you gave him the phone?"

Again, he'd ignored her question. It was starting to irritate her. "He did say something. But I didn't catch it. Someone started talking over one of the bullhorns and drowned out his words. But I got the impression that he was going to give the phone to someone."

Neither man looked happy about that news. They exchanged a glance.

"Why? What's the matter?"

Detective Packard leaned toward her. "Did you see him speaking to anyone? It's important."

"Pack." Detective Lexington's voice held a note that indicated his partner should back off.

Camryn felt the blood drain from her face. "Wait. What did you just say?"

The detectives looked at her blankly.

"You called him Pack."

Detective Lexington nodded.

Camryn squeezed her temples between thumb and fingers. "That must have been what he meant."

"What who meant?"

"The man. The undercover officer who was hit by the car. He kept saying, 'Pack police.' But I didn't understand what that meant." Her eyes widened and she lifted her gaze to Detective Packard. "I think he wanted me to give *you* the phone."

The two men exchanged another grim look.

Detective Packard drummed his thumbs on the tabletop, deep in thought. After a moment he said, "You couldn't have known. Did you tell that to officer Skelly, though? About him saying 'Pack police?'"

She nodded her head. "Yes. But he didn't seem to know what it meant."

"And back to my earlier question. Did you see who Skelly spoke with after he left you with the phone?"

"No. I'm sorry. I'd just worked a twelve-hour shift. I think I shut my eyes until that other officer got in."

Detective Packard sank against the back of his chair with a sigh.

Camryn searched their faces for what she might be missing.

Detective Lexington drew a hand over his forehead and back through his hair—a gesture that revealed his weariness.

She wondered how many hours he'd worked in a row.

He gave her a resigned shrug. "Officer Skelly has been killed. We only got the word a few minutes ago. You were the last one to speak to him, other than— Well, we were hoping you might have some information for us."

Camryn felt the words as though a pail of ice water had been tossed in her face. He'd seemed like such a kind and caring man.

Without another word, Detective Packard pushed from the table and left the room.

Detective Lexington stood, but hesitated. "I'm sorry to ask this, but we need you to stay here for a little longer."

She felt her brow pinch. "I have to be to work at eight." She hated it when they made her work back to back shifts at the opposite ends of a workday, but she couldn't afford to take any time off.

Detective Lexington was already shaking his head. "For your own safety, I don't think you should go to work today."

Camryn's heartrate ratcheted up a couple notches. "Listen, I have bills to pay. I can't afford—" Realization of what he'd just said penetrated. "My own safety?"

"I'll explain more in a few minutes. For now, stay here. We'll be back." With that, he left the room.

For her own safety? Camryn gripped the edge of the table, willing herself to remain calm. So much for thinking that God might finally be answering her prayers.

How had her life changed so drastically in the space of one day?

Chapter 6

Damien planted his fists on his desk and leaned into them, head hanging.

Lexington was sure making a racket over at his desk.

He lifted his head. His partner was madly gathering papers and statements and stuffing them into an unmarked three-ring binder. He stabbed a finger in Damien's direction and spoke low. "Gather the interviews you filled out and print out the pictures you took at the scene. Then copy those interview recordings onto a thumb-drive and give it here. Do it now. I'll record the 911 call onto a thumb-drive."

Damien frowned. Maybe it was the fact that they were going on hour twenty-four without any sleep, but had Case gone out of his mind? "What are you talking about?" All he could think about was what might have been on that phone, meant for him, and bad enough that it had likely gotten not only Treyvon killed, but Skelly as well.

Case stepped close and gripped him by one arm, giving him a little shake. When he spoke, his words were so soft Damien could barely hear them. But what they lacked in volume, they certainly made up for in intensity. "Wake up, Damien! There are dirty cops in *our* precinct. Ones that weren't afraid to go so far as to kill a fellow officer. I have a family to think about now. We have to play this smart, not hard. Our only chance of outsmarting these guys is to—"

"Get copies of this evidence into a safe place that only you and I know about."

Case looked relieved to finally have him back on board. "Yes. After that, then we can try to figure out what Treyvon might have been trying to send you on that phone."

A new surge of energy swept in to fill the void that his brief wallow in grief had created. "We have to get that girl into protective custody too. Especially if Miller was trying to take her from the scene."

Case nodded gravely. "He was. And I know just the guy to help us with her." Case leveled him with a pointed look. "He's on his way here with Skelly's remains."

Damien snapped his fingers. "Yes. He's perfect."

"First, we copy all the evidence. Meet me back there in five minutes." Case stabbed a finger toward the room where the witness still waited.

As Case stepped to his desk and plugged in a thumb drive, Damien tapped steepled fingers against his lips. Miller had been at the top of their suspect list for months. They'd had strong suspicions that he was a dirty cop. But with the way the union worked, the captain said they didn't have enough evidence to be actionable.

Six months ago, he and Lexington were handed a case where an elderly woman had been beaten and raped in her home. Miller, new to the force at the time, had been the first on the scene. He claimed he'd arrived after the 911 call, which had been placed by the victim's husband, a man with the beginnings of dementia from what they could tell when they interviewed him. Miller had claimed that a man wearing a black ski mask had been fleeing the premises. But by the time Damien and Lexington had concluded their investigation, they'd both been convinced that Miller had taken part in the crime—or at the very least had looked the other way and helped the crook escape. But they'd never been able to get proof. With the husband's mental decline, he'd given multiple versions of the incident that were just different enough not to be trustworthy. Their hopes had been on getting a statement from the victim herself, but she'd been in a coma. For three days, they hoped she'd be able to tell them more when she came around, but she'd passed away without waking.

Damien loosed a breath and got to work copying pages. It grated on him that such a man was still on the force, but if the tables were turned, he'd want due process in his own favor. Besides, it seemed pretty clear that Miller was not working alone. Key evidence against him had turned up missing on two further occasions. He obviously had some help on the inside, but they had no idea who it might be.

What they did know was that things had been haywire around here for months. Besides the evidence going missing, CI's had been outed on two occasions in the past three months, with deadly results. And now in the span of an hour, two police officers had been killed—one undercover and one investigating his murder.

Treyvon had obviously stumbled onto something big. Something that had made him come out from his cover. But if Trey hadn't had time to tell anyone what he'd learned, why had Skelly been killed? Was there something he knew that he shouldn't have known? Or was there some connection between the two men that Damien wasn't aware of? And why had Trey wanted *him* to have his phone? Other than training him that very first day, he'd hardly known the kid.

Damien snatched up the notes from the interview with the waitress.

The phone. That had to be it. The waitress had given it to Skelly and he'd obviously taken it to someone. But the waitress said she hadn't heard what he said. Whoever he'd taken that phone to... Had that been what cost him his life? But why? The phone had been smashed, she'd said. So presumably Skelly hadn't been able to listen to or view anything on it. But if that were true, it made no sense that he'd been killed.

It was all such a puzzle.

"Heard you two are working Treyvon Johnson's case?"

Damien glanced up to see a lab-tech standing next to his desk with a small sheaf of papers.

"Yeah. What's up?"

The man held out the pages. "Thought you should know that Ryan Skelly's computer in his vehicle was wiped clean."

Damien grunted. That was odd. "Nothing?"

The tech shook his head. "Totally wiped. Zeroed out every last sector."

Damien sighed.

The tech started away but then paused. "There is one anomaly that might be pertinent to your case."

"Oh?"

The man nudged his glasses up his nose. "I noticed a glitch on the station servers this morning. The audit logs show a deletion outside of business hours that was flagged by anomaly detection due to the source IP being unrecognized. The operation succeeded despite detection, and unfortunately the differential and daily backups are also missing."

Damien reached for his cup. "What?" He slugged down another shot of caffeine. He was going to need it to follow this conversation.

"It looks like it was an outsider with inside knowledge, or we may be dealing with an otherwise undetected APT."

"I need this in plain English."

The tech grumbled something under his breath, then said, "Something that was sent to the station servers was deleted sometime in the night, most likely by someone with inside knowledge."

"Can you tell what it was?"

The tech shook his head. "Sorry. Unrecoverable."

"So what you're telling me is that Skelly may have sent something to the station servers from his vehicle, but that both his vehicle computer and the information on the servers have been deleted?"

The tech pondered. "I suppose they could be related. But..." He shrugged. "Unprovable."

Unprovable.

So far that summed up almost everything about this case. Except of course for the two dead bodies.

The helicopter banked toward the city of Everett as it approached from the westerly San Juan Islands. From his position in the back seat, Holden adjusted the noise cancelling headset and took in the coral wash of the sunrise to the east. With the dark mounds of green islands dotting the dawn-blue waters of the Puget Sound and the first rays of the golden sun reflecting off the windows of the downtown hospital, he could have almost felt like he was on a pleasure cruise were it not for his grim task.

They had bagged the bucket containing the officer's remains and then put it on ice in a sealed cooler. It was strapped in beside him. A grim reminder that this wasn't a sightseeing jaunt.

The large H on top of the police headquarters building beckoned them ever nearer. The fact that Jay had his chopper license was one of the reasons that Holden had liked his resume so much and had been the deciding factor in hiring the young deputy—despite rumors that pervaded the island about Holden only hiring him due to the connection between their relatives.

As the chopper landed, Holden reached for a pair of latex gloves and tugged them on. "Just wait for me. I won't be long."

Jay nodded.

Cooler in hand, Holden ducked to avoid the wind of the decelerating propeller blades as he hurried toward the officer holding the door open for him across the roof. The man didn't look like he should be much past milk-drinking, much less a cop. Were they deputizing teenagers these days? Holden pressed his lips together. Maybe he was just getting older.

"You Parker?" the officer hollered above the noise.

Holden nodded.

The kid's gaze dipped to the cooler and his face paled visibly. "This way!"

Holden followed through several empty hallways until they stepped into the main part of the police office. He frowned. Normally an office like this would be filled with the clack of keyboards, the clanking of handcuffs, and the chatter of conversation, but except for a few people the place was nearly empty.

The young officer turned to face him. "Lexington and Packard are there at their desks." He pointed. "I can take...*that* down to the ME's office, if you want."

He could have dressed the kid down, but decided against it. This was a rough day for everyone. The kid was probably doing good simply to keep his wits together, much less consider nuances like the fact that the fewer steps in a chain of evidence there were, the better. "I'll take it down myself. I just want to let them know I've arrived."

The kid shrugged. "Suit yourself."

Packard and Lexington were already striding toward him.

"You made it." Case gave him a friendly thump on one shoulder.

Packard simply gave him a nod.

Holden quirked a brow. "Kind of quiet around here?"

Lexington nodded. "There's been an escape over at SCJ."

Damien slashed a hand of dismissal that cut further questions short. "We need to talk before you leave."

"I'll be back up as soon as I drop this off."

"Meet us in the interrogation room off the deputy chief's office." Damien pointed across the way. "And"—he leaned closer and lowered his voice—"keep the witness in there as out of sight as possible."

Holden's brows lifted at that. He glanced again toward the interrogation room and noted that the blinds on the room's only window were closed from the inside and there was no door to that room from out here. A person could only enter if they were in the deputy chief's office. He knew better than to ask questions out here in the main room, but if they were trying to keep a witness out of sight, it could only mean that they didn't trust some of their fellow officers.

"Go right in when you get back." Case pointed out the sign to the ME's office. "We're finalizing a few things and will be in as soon as we can."

Camryn made circles with the paper cup that was now a quarter full of stone-cold coffee. She had her speech all planned for when they came back and told her once more that she couldn't go to work. Surely, they would understand that she was trying to dig her way out from under the mound of bills. And she hadn't seen anything other than what she'd told them. The little that she'd seen couldn't be grounds for someone to wish her harm, could it? She'd simply been minding her own business on her way home from work. That was what she wanted to get back to—minding her own business.

The doorknob jostled.

Oh good. Here they were now.

A blond man she'd never seen before stepped swiftly through the door and snapped it closed behind him.

She lurched to her feet, knocking the cup over. The chill of the rear wall resisted her spine, trapping her in the room with the stranger. She pressed one hand to her thumping chest.

The man's hands shot to shoulder height, palms out. "Sorry to startle you. I don't mean you any harm."

Only a fraction of her alarm dissipated. "Who are you?" She took note of his uniform, which was different from those she normally saw on officers around here. One arm of a dark brown shirt that stretched taut over broad shoulders displayed a patch that read "Sheriff." Her scrutiny swept down to a pair of medium brown slacks that hung from trim hips and then rebounded to the day's-worth of scruff that coated his pleasantly masculine jawline and the vivid blue eyes that returned her scrutiny.

She worked some moisture into her mouth. He might be nice to look at, but with his size and fitness, if he wanted to harm her, she was a goner.

He glanced at the mess she'd made on the table and reached for one of the napkins Detective Lexington had left in a stack. As he sopped up the mess, he said, "I'm Sheriff Holden Parker. I work out on San Juan Island."

With his focus elsewhere, she allowed her gaze to trail once more over the pleasant cut of his shoulders. "Work out" was obviously correct. She withheld a smirk at her own pathetic humor and reminded herself she still wasn't sure if she could trust him. "And what are you doing here?"

He lifted her a look. "I'm here on the job, ma'am."

Ma'am? He made her sound like an aged spinster. But after the night she'd had, maybe she looked like one. "I mean here in this interrogation room."

He deposited the soaking wet napkins in a trash can by the door and used another to dry the last of the spill. "Detectives Packard and Lexington asked me to wait in here with you."

"Why?"

His lips tilted into the barest hint of a smile. "They'll be along shortly. I'm sure they'll tell us then." He tossed the last of the trash, including her cup, into the waste bin and then folded his arms and leaned into his heels. "You can sit back down if you want."

Normally she was a trusting person, but today all her caution was on full alert. "I'm fine."

"Suit yourself." He lifted one shoulder. "You never gave me your name."

"Camryn. Camryn Hunt. Do you think I could use a restroom?"

"Sure. The deputy chief has a private one. Let me just close the main door." He left the interrogation room and returned a few seconds later. "Coast is clear."

She stepped into the cluttered deputy chief's office with its private restroom on the other side. After she used the facilities and washed her hands, she stood before the mirror and stretched her neck and back.

She pulled a face at herself. With her messy bun looking more like "rat's nest" than "shabby chic" and the blue-gray bags beneath her eyes, no wonder the handsome sheriff called her 'ma'am.' She looked ten years older. She splashed some water on her face and quickly re-bound her hair.

It felt so good to be standing, instead of returning immediately to the interrogation room, she wandered the perimeter of the deputy chief's office, taking in the pictures on his walls. There was a large painting of an old English fox hunt behind his desk and several plaques of commendations and medals he'd won.

She heard a sound behind her and turned.

It was the sheriff. "I don't think they want you out here," he said. "They're trying to keep you from being seen." He nodded toward the main office.

Before she had the opportunity to respond the door opened to admit the detectives. Each man carried a cardboard file box. Their eyes widened at the sight of her and they quickly shut the door to the main office.

Officer Lexington jutted his chin toward the inner room. "Let's go back in there, if you don't mind."

Camryn sighed, but didn't protest. She followed the sheriff back to the stainless-steel table.

The detectives set their boxes on the table and closed the door.

Camryn opened her mouth to inform them that she really needed to get to work, but Detective Lexington raised a hand.

He lifted an item that looked like a pen from his pocket and gave it a twist. "Okay, now we can talk freely." Camryn must have had a blank look on her face, because he explained, "It scrambles signals so any listening device has a harder time picking up our words."

Camryn didn't miss the way Sheriff Parker straightened.

"A listening device?" she asked.

Detective Packard waved a hand. "For now, it's just a precaution. We don't want what we have to say now getting to the wrong ears."

Camryn felt her jaw go slack. What in the world had she gotten herself into? How had she gone from a day of peddling burgers and shakes to a night of covert conversations protected by spy gadgets?

The sheriff's voice emerged gruffly. "I take it you have dirty cops in your division?"

Packard gripped the back of his neck. "We're afraid so. Still trying to figure how all the pieces fit together."

Lexington kept his gaze on the sheriff but swept a gesture in Camryn's direction. "You used to work in major crimes and have experience with WP. We need—"

"What's WP?" Camryn interrupted.

"—your help to keep her safe. She needs to leave town for...I don't know...at least until we can get a better handle on what's going on around here."

"Leave town!" Camryn's dismay emerged on a squeak and she felt her cheeks warm. "Listen, I have bills to pay and I can't—"

"Your life is more important than bills." All three men spoke in unison, as though they had rehearsed.

The sheriff gave her an understanding glance. "WP is witness protection. It's never undertaken lightly. Only when law enforcement believes a person is in grave danger."

Her shoulders slumped. She massaged her temples. How had she come to be a witness in a case such as this? "I was just walking to the bus stop."

Detective Lexington dipped his chin. "I know. And I'm sorry to yank the rug out from under your life, but until we know exactly what's going on, we need to keep you safe. These men have already killed two police officers."

"But I don't know anything other than what I've told you!"

"Yes, ma'am. But these kinds of men, they live in worlds where they can't afford to leave any loose ends. They won't hesitate to take you out. Even if they only *fear* you know too much. Do you have family? Kids? A husband? Pets?"

She shook her head no to each question, feeling like she'd been pressured into running a marathon without training and was trying to keep up. "No."

"Good that will simplify things."

The two detectives looked at Sheriff Parker, brows raised.

Camryn sank into the chair she'd vacated a few minutes ago. She propped her head on one hand.

Sheriff Parker shuffled his feet. "I've got a place I could stash her, yeah."

Great. They could "stash" her. Like a box on a shelf in a closet. Forgotten until the end of time. Okay, maybe that was a bit melodramatic.

"Good." Detective Packard gave his box a pat. "We need you to keep these records for us too."

The sheriff eyed the boxes. "Do I get to look at the files?"

"Actually, we were kind of hoping you would. Maybe you'll see what we haven't all this time. There's something we are missing here."

"I'm happy to take a look. But to pull this off, we're going to need a second waitress."

"A second waitress?" Detective Lexington asked.

Camryn was just as confused.

The sheriff nodded. "If I fly out of here with her, everyone in the precinct is going to know she's in hiding on the islands. I don't want to invite that kind of trouble on my people." He looked at Lexington. "Isn't your wife into theatrical stuff? Seem to remember her disguising herself when you worked that drug case out on San Juan last year."

"She is. I'll get her."

"Excuse me. Don't I get a say in whether I want to be protected or not?"

"Good." The sheriff didn't even glance her way. He looked at Packard. "Can you find me a trustworthy female officer, about her height, coloring, and weight?" He jabbed a finger in Camryn's direction.

She tossed one hand in the air and flopped against the back of her seat.

Packard pondered. "There's a rookie who fits the bill. She's only been here two days and been doing entry paperwork for most of that. I don't think that's long enough to be corrupted."

"Even better because most of the other officers won't know what she looks like. Is she on duty?"

Packard nodded. "Should be. I'll get her."

"Get your captain to assign her TDY to my department. We can say I need her for...a twenty-four-seven security detail of a celebrity."

Detective Packard waved his acknowledgement. "Cap's down at the jail right now. But I'll write up the paperwork and have him sign it tomorrow." He stepped from the room.

It was once more only her and the sheriff.

He sat across from her and bounced his forehead against steepled fingers, deep in thought.

Camryn glowered at the top of his head. "All of this is ridiculous."

He didn't look up. "If we let you go back to your own place and you...become another victim, that's on us. Most people have no idea the depths these kinds of criminals will go to."

Somehow the little pause in the middle of his sentence made her realize exactly what he *wasn't* saying.

If she didn't listen to them, she *would* end up dead like the officers.

She sighed.

Put like that, did she have any choice but to do as they asked?

Chapter 7

An hour later, Holden watched as the detectives hustled the female officer through the growing bustle of the precinct. Several units were still hunting for the escapee, apparently, but several more had returned to their duties at the precinct. And that would work in their favor.

The female officer had now been transformed into the spitting image of Miss Hunt, complete with waitress uniform and apron, and he was pleased to see that plenty of the officers took note of her leaving.

"Hey Pack," one of them called. "Where you taking her?"

Damien waved a hand. "Stick to your own case, Ed."

Ed's lips thinned. He didn't like being told to mind his own business. But the interaction had been exactly what Holden had hoped for. Drew enough attention that every man in the room thought the witness from the night before was being removed from the building.

Thankfully, most of these officers hadn't been on shift the evening before to see what she looked like. And if any of them had been at the scene, maybe the darkness and chaos had kept them from getting a good look at her.

He turned to assess Camryn, who paced behind the interrogation table. It was amazing what Case's wife had been able to do with her appearance. Kyra Lexington had arrived at the precinct on the pretense of bringing her husband breakfast since he hadn't come home the evening before. Case snuck her in here. And from the amount of makeup she'd dumped from her paper McDonald's bag, it was a wonder the bag hadn't torn.

But the transformation she'd completed on the waitress was incredible. It was amazing how much a little makeup could change someone's appearance. Her face looked thinner, forehead longer—just like the rookie. Somehow with a few brush strokes she'd made over one woman into another so that only those who knew them best would be able to tell them apart.

Camryn hitched up the duty belt that didn't tighten quite enough to fit her slender hips. "Can we go now? You are at least going to let me stop by my place to get some things, aren't you?" She hefted her coat. "And bring my coat?"

He narrowed his eyes at her. She'd been instructed not to talk after Case turned off the scrambler, but he supposed her words could have just as easily been asked by a deputy assigned to temporary duty in his department.

She rolled her eyes and tugged at the uniform sleeves that were too long for her. Hopefully they would get through the precinct quickly enough that no one would notice the ill fit. As for her coat, the chopper ride could get a little chilly this time of year. It would be good for her to have it. He opened one of the cardboard filing boxes and compressed all the files to one end, then motioned for her coat, which he flattened as much as possible and then shoved into the box before replacing the lid.

He checked the scene from the deputy chief's office. Lexington and Packard had already disappeared through the far door. He pointed Miss Hunt toward the door with his chin, indicating it was go-time. She didn't move. He hoped the look he gave her conveyed support before he nudged her into the main office with the file boxes against her back.

He spoke in a normal tone of voice. "Glad to have you serving with us for a couple weeks, Hewlett. On the island every officer has to pull a lot of weight, but this protective detail would have had us stretched really thin. We appreciate your help."

"Yes, sir. Happy to help, sir." Her voice emerged steadily without even a hint of a tremor.

Good for her. The woman had some chops.

Holden looked up and was both gratified and terrified to find almost every eye in the room on them. Could they pull this off? Was anyone going to recognize that she was not the new rookie? He stepped out. "Helo is this way."

Most everyone turned back to their own business.

Camryn followed him with a purposeful stride.

He kept to a good clip, thankful to hear the soft tread of her boots keeping time with him.

It had been a bold plan, but his first training officer had told him once if not a thousand times, "If you're going to create a lie, make it loud and bold, and hardly anyone will pause to think twice."

He could only hope that was the case this time.

Camryn had never gotten to ride in a helicopter before, and the scenery sweeping along below them took her breath away. She wished she wasn't feeling so disgruntled and discombobulated. With a determined clench of her jaw, she resolved not to let her weariness and fears of the future overcome her enjoyment of this experience.

The cerulean blue of the Pacific contrasted with the emerald and taupe mounds of the San Juan Islands. Off to the north, the great snowy mound of Mount Baker floated on a bank of clouds as though it hovered above the ground. Despite the helo doors being firmly shut, a biting chill in the cabin cut through the flimsy fabric of the police uniform reminding her once more that she hadn't been allowed to pick up even one item from her apartment. She cut a churlish look at the sheriff beside her as she reached into the box at her feet, extracted her coat, and put it on.

It might all be well and good for him to say they would get her new clothes and toiletries once they arrived on the island, but she honestly didn't have the money to spend on new clothes right now. And especially not from shops that were likely a lot more expensive due to the tourist nature of the islands.

The sheriff nudged her arm and spoke through the headset. "Look." He gestured to the water below his side of the helicopter.

She leaned toward him, placing one hand against the back of his seat to look through his window.

A group of seals cavorted and frolicked around a green buoy, clearly visible even when they were below the surface of the water.

She pulled in a breath of awe.

The sheriff caught the pilot's attention and circled a finger in the air. When they'd first climbed aboard, Sheriff Parker had introduced the man as Deputy Jay Powers. The deputy nodded and banked the helicopter into a circle above the seals.

For several minutes they flew in a holding pattern, enjoying the sight of three seals breaching and diving. One would sun itself on the buoy platform until another would launch out of the water and vie for a position in the warmth, knocking the first one off. Bright sunlight glistened off the black of water-sluiced heads. Finally, all three seals managed to balance precariously on the lip of the platform, heads resting against each other's tails like a circle of napping puppies.

"They are so cute!" Camryn tossed the sheriff a glance, only to see that he was no longer watching the seals, but had transferred his gaze to her.

Smile lines crinkled the corners of his eyes, drawing her attention to the nicest pair of silvery blues she'd ever had the pleasure to encounter. Flecks of light blue contrasted starkly with the black of his pupils and the darker blue at the outer edges of his irises. With his blond curls and the sketch of a golden beard highlighting the angular planes of his jaw, he was like a piece of art. She could stare at this particular sculpture all day and never tire.

Warmth blazed through her cheeks. She cleared her throat and resettled herself into the distance of her own seat.

He got Deputy Powers' attention. "We should get going."

The man gave a little salute of acknowledgement and banked the chopper around into a straight course toward the northwest again.

She watched the scenery for a few minutes until she felt the sheriff bat her arm with the back of his hand.

"You ever rappelled before?" he asked.

Camryn frowned. What an odd question. She must not have heard him right. She pressed the bulky headphones tighter to her head. "What was that?"

"Rappelling? Ever done it before?"

She felt her frown deepen. "Like repelled people? I mean, I try to be kind, so I hope not, but I suppose there's a possibility—"

He chuckled and shared a look of amusement with the pilot.

Her confusion mounted. "What?"

"I'm going to take your answer to mean no. Rappelling is lowering yourself from a height. In this case, from a helicopter that isn't on the ground."

Her eyes shot wide. "We can't land on the island?"

"The only landing pad is at the airport, but to keep people from knowing you are on the island, we will go straight to The Cabin."

She glanced at the deputy. "What about him?"

The sheriff's words resonated with truth when he said, "I'd trust him with my life."

She pondered on that. So for her own protection she was going to have to risk her life by jumping out of a flying helicopter? "Won't people notice the helicopter hovering over your property?"

He shrugged. "Not likely. I own twenty acres, and Jay owns the acreage just to my north. My other neighbor works on the mainland and doesn't get back home till evening. Besides, we'll only need to hover for a few seconds. A minute tops."

Her mouth went dry. He really and truly expected her to jump. "I think I'd rather we landed at the airport. I'll take the risk."

He shook his head. "Everything will be fine. I'll have you the whole way down, but we need to get geared up." He reached into a compartment below his seat, then handed her a contraption that looked like an oversized dog harness.

She held it up, stretched it out, twisted it around, trying to figure out what went where.

"Like this." He unstrapped his seat harness and stood, motioning for her to follow him into the space behind their seats in the back of the helo.

With a glance toward the pilot, she followed the sheriff's example. If the pilot made any sudden course changes, she was going to end up crashing into the side walls of this thing.

By putting his own harness on, the sheriff demonstrated the correct method for donning hers. "Leg's through here. These straps go over your shoulders."

She followed his instructions to the letter and fastened the last buckle with a feeling of accomplishment, but he didn't seem satisfied. He stepped right into her personal space and tugged and adjusted the straps of the harness. He was all business, but nonetheless, she felt her face heat and looked away as his hands circled behind her, still tugging and fine-tuning.

He was so close she caught a whiff of an alluring cologne that made her want to lean close for a deeper inhale. Heavens, she needed to keep in mind what was going on here. The man had been assigned to keep her alive. This wasn't some crazy date in a gorgeous island location. The very fact that she was about to jump out of a perfectly good helicopter ought to drive that realization home.

Finally, he seemed satisfied that she was properly harnessed. "Ready?"

She spread her hands. "Do I have a choice?"

One corner of his mouth tipped up. "We're five minutes out. When the time comes, we'll go out that door." He pointed to the one on his side of the chopper. All you have to do is lean into me and relax, I'll do all the work, got it?"

She twisted her fingers together. "You're sure we can't just land at the airport? I'll even let you put me in the trunk so no one will see me in the car."

He reached out and squeezed her arm. "To do that I'd need someone to bring over a car. In a small community like this, word of your presence would spread like wildfire."

Drat, but she felt her fear climbing up to take over and she wasn't even near the door of the chopper yet. "Couldn't I pretend to be the rookie officer you dressed me up as?"

He shook his head. "Too dangerous." His throat worked and there was a flash of pain in his eyes. "You don't have the training you need. I'm trying to protect you, not put you in dangerous situations."

"Except for making me jump out of a helicopter."

He smiled, drawing her attention to two stubbled dimples on either side of his lips. "You'll be perfectly safe, I promise."

She pulled her gaze from his face. Maybe she'd be perfectly safe in body, but what about in heart after this stint on the islands? And what had that flash of pain in his gaze been all about?

"We're here." The pilot's voice crackled over their headsets.

The sheriff pressed the lever on the side door and slid the door open with a clang. Treetops along the island's shore whipped by, and then they stopped above a small flat clearing.

The chopper lowered until it hovered right above the treetops. But these were towering hundred foot tall trees, not your average backyard variety. And the clearing they were apparently aiming for didn't look much larger than a postage stamp—okay, maybe an envelope. But what if the wind caught them and swept them into the trees? Or worse yet, the water? If Sheriff Parker was irritated at her fear of jumping from the craft, she couldn't imagine what he'd feel if he understood her sheer terror of water.

Memory flashed. The beautiful blue of the neighborhood pool. The cool tiles beneath her toes as water sloshed all around her. The warmth of the sun beating down on her head and shoulders as she played and splashed with her best friend. The shadow that had blocked out the sun for a split second before the hand settled on the top of her head. With a shudder, she shook the memory away.

Nausea roiled and the floor of the helicopter seemed to tilt, though the helicopter hadn't changed angles. She groped to steady herself on the sheriff's seat.

"Hey." He once more stepped into her space. This time he touched her chin. He searched her face. "Stay with me here. This will all be over in thirty seconds, all right? Just close your eyes and trust me."

"And pray like mad?"

He chuckled as he tugged on a pair of leather gloves. "Yeah, you can do that too."

Just great. Her last hope was prayer? She wasn't sure why she'd even mentioned it.

He kicked a large pile of rope from the door, and for the first time she noted the huge crimp of metal that held one end of the rope firmly in the ceiling of the chopper. "Ready?"

She swallowed. Forced herself to nod. "We aren't going near the water, are we?" She couldn't stop a tremor.

By his sweeping gaze, he must have noticed her trembling, but he only offered, "Nowhere near the water. Here we go." He stepped close behind her and did something with her harness. She heard the snap of metal and felt tension against her shoulder straps as he clicked something that linked them together. "Back with me toward the door."

She complied, heart in her throat. *Think happy thoughts. Feet walking on a street. Backside pressed firmly to a soft bench. Curled up comfortably in her recliner, safely on the ground.* All very happy tho—

"Here we go." The sheriff launched himself backward out of the helicopter, dragging her with him.

She jolted. Her eyes shot open. She was dangling in front of the sheriff like a kid in a baby carrier. She scrabbled to grab the rope. But it was behind her, between her and the sheriff.

"Steady." His voice soothed through her headset. "I've got you. Almost over."

Despite his reassuring words they were part grunt, like a man doing hard labor and speaking at the same time. And she realized that her flailing was likely making things harder for him. She caught a brief glimpse of blue ocean dotted with green islands, and then they slid into the canopy of the treetops.

It was only moments later that their feet touched down. The tension on her harness released as the sheriff unclasped her from him.

She stepped to one side and sank into a crouch. *Good old terra-firma.* The ground was frozen and a few dustings of snow lay against the base of tree trunks where today's sun apparently hadn't touched.

"See?" The sheriff grinned. "God answered your prayers."

She rolled her eyes. "Actually, I'm not really much of a prayer anymore."

The sheriff didn't seem fazed by her reply. He gave the rope a snap to distance it from them and then gave the pilot a thumbs up.

Through the window of the chopper, the deputy returned a two-fingered salute and flew off with the rope still dangling from the side-door.

Camryn frowned and willed herself to breathe and cease trembling. "Won't people who see it wonder why the rope is out?"

The sheriff was already at work removing his harness. "Maybe. But curiosity and questions we can handle. It's the eyewitness rumors that I'd like to avoid. Besides, you'd be surprised at the number of people around here who don't even bother looking up at the sound of a plane or helicopter going over. They come and go all the time." He thumbed a gesture over his shoulder. "The Cabin is this way." He strode off up the hill. "So you used to pray?"

"What?" Camryn rose from her squat and followed him.

"You said *anymore*. 'I'm not really much of a prayer, anymore.'"

"Right. Yes. I used to pray. Often." Her legs still felt as weak as a newborn's, but at least she'd survived the jump from the chopper.

"I see."

She held her breath, waiting for him to probe and pondering how she could skirt the looming questions. But they never came. He simply led the way quietly on a narrow trail.

Huh. Maybe the man was not only good-looking but knew when to mind his own business too. At least if she had to be here hiding out, that was something to be thankful for. If only she didn't have so many looming bills, she could almost enjoy spending a couple weeks in this beautiful location. Especially with a man like that.

She rolled her eyes at herself. She needed to remember this was temporary and that he was only performing a duty. Repeating the thought to herself until it was firmly embedded in her conscience, she gave a nod of satisfaction.

But her gaze betrayed her and wandered to the man lithely leading her through the towering evergreens. My... She let herself take in the angular line from his broad shoulders to his trim waist. If she had to be confined, at least it was with someone easy on the eyes.

She forced her focus to the path at her feet.

Temporary. Only duty. Temporary. Only duty. Temporary. Only duty.

Chapter 8

Holden led the woman from the shore level up the hill behind his house, taking the natural-cut stone steps that were framed with borders of moss. The back patio was made in the same style—a broad swath of natural flagstones, interspersed with green moss.

"This is your 'cabin'?" The awe in her voice made him pause to take in the grandeur of the river-rock that accented the wall of windows overlooking the channel.

"Used to be my grandparent's place. Grandma was all about architecture that blended with the nature around it. Grandpa always called it The Cabin. I suppose that's why I generally do too. And grandma finally had a sign made."

"It's amazing. Are those hand-hewn stones framing the windows?"

"Yeah. Actually, those were chiseled from a huge rock that was right here on the property. They had to blast it to make room for the house. Gran was so pleased to frame the arches of the windows and doorways with stone cut right out of this land."

"Amazing." She turned to face the water and gave a gasp of delight.

He followed her gaze past the trunks of the evergreens to the vibrant blues of the Salish Sea and greens of Orcas and Shaw Islands floating in the distance. The Victoria BC ferry was headed north at the moment, and majestic Mount Baker, newly dressed in a cloak of glistening snow, capped the distance like a benevolent queen overlooking her realm.

He really needed to pause more often to take it all in. He lived in one of the most beautiful places on earth, but it had become the norm.

He let his gaze wander to her once more. Tendrils of dark hair had come loose from the tight police bun that Kyra Lexington had pinned up only an hour ago. The wind set them to dancing around her face. She reached up to tuck one behind her ear, her gaze still transfixed on the scenery.

Beautiful, and younger than he'd thought when he first saw her. Despite her original reluctance to go into hiding, once she caved to their admonitions, she hadn't resisted anything he asked her to do... Well, except maybe when he dragged her from the chopper. He rubbed away a smirk. She'd showed real courage in a difficult situation.

He swallowed and looked away. He couldn't forget that he was on the job. He couldn't let this turn into another Traci.

His stomach recoiled at the thought.

"You're afraid of water?" Even if the blurted question was more about getting his thoughts moving in another direction, he regretted it the moment it left his lips.

She seemed to curl in on herself. Arms folded. Shoulders hunched. Focus no longer on the scenery, but on prodding gently with one boot at a swatch of moss in the seam between two flagstones. "It's a bit chilly out here. Do you mind if we go inside?"

"Of course." He was an idiot. "I'll show you to your room and get you a change of clothes." What was he going to give her to wear? He didn't have any women's clothes, but he couldn't expect her to keep wearing that uniform.

He showed her to the guest room on the east side of the second floor with the best view of the water. "There's an attached bathroom there, and if you need extra pillows or blankets, you'll find them on the top shelf in the closet. Give me five minutes and I'll bring you a change of clothes. Then you can rest or shower or whatever you'd like to do, while I cook us some lunch."

She glanced at her watch. "Is it really only lunch time? I feel like I could sleep for weeks."

He assessed the weariness in her posture. "You've had a hard couple of days."

She pulled a face. "Not as hard as some."

"Yeah. There's that." He massaged the muscles of his shoulders, for a moment lost in thought about the two officers who'd been killed.

She shuffled her feet.

He jolted back to the present. "Be right back. You can wait on the balcony if you want."

In his room down the hall, he rummaged through his drawers until he came up with the smallest pair of sweatpants he owned. They would be too big, but at least they had a drawstring. He yanked a Seahawks jersey out of his closet and returned down the hall.

He found her leaning on the rail on the balcony. "These are the best I can do for right now. I'll get you some clothes in town tomorrow."

She accepted the sweatpants and shirt. "How are you going to pass off buying women's clothes? Won't that raise questions on the island?"

"Yeah, it will. I'm honestly still working on that."

"Does Amazon deliver out here?"

Holden snapped his fingers. "That's perfect."

She shrugged. "With their Prime delivery, that might be the best solution."

"Out here we get most of our packages via drones. The landing pad is out front."

"Wow. A lot has changed from when we were kids, hasn't it?"

"Sure has." He saw a look of worry flash into her eyes. "What is it?"

She clutched the clothes to her chest with one arm and swept a lock of hair behind her ear with the other hand. "It's nothing. Don't worry about it. I'll figure it out."

Realization dawned. She was tight on funds. "Hey, this is on the department dime."

"It is?" Her brows rose.

Thrusting his hands into his pockets to keep from reaching out to give her arm a reassuring squeeze, he nodded. "It is. They wouldn't let you go home to collect your things, so they'll cover reasonable expenses."

A quirk tugged at her lips. "You mean a Ferrari is out?"

He chuckled. "Yeah. That's probably a no go. Not sure Amazon delivers those, anyhow. At least not by drone."

An exaggerated snap of her fingers accompanied her chuckle. "Drat."

"Meet me in the kitchen in forty-five minutes?"

She tilted her head. "Is it hard to find?"

"Not at all. Downstairs. North end of the house."

Confusion crinkled her brow.

"That end." He pointed.

"Right. Yes. See you then."

As he left her in her room and headed downstairs, he couldn't help but think once more how much this whole situation reminded him of the one with Traci. And the realization that they were similar was enough to raise his pulse in terror.

Dear God, please don't let me fail twice.

Just the thought was enough to armor his heart.

No matter how attractive and personable she was, he couldn't let feelings get in the way of duty.

The pier of the Everett marina swayed lazily with the undulation of the water as Soren Bane strode toward a small yacht with his two bodyguards trailing. The air was chilly today. The wind cut through his silk suit like a blade.

It irritated him to be here.

If people would simply do what they were paid to do, this meeting wouldn't be necessary. But of course, conservatives were all products of a broken, Stone Age system that needed to be torn down from the inside out, and they just couldn't see it. Restructuring was the only way real money could be made.

Yes, they were all mindless idiots, but if he had to work with one in order to get to the end goal of destroying them all, so be it.

He just didn't like meeting in broad daylight like this.

The boat creaked as he left his bodyguards on the pier and stepped onto the deck. The aft stairs led down to the cabin.

Republican State Senator Carter Cranston was already there, lounging on the leather bench seat with a glass in one hand.

That gave Soren pause. He hadn't seen the man's bodyguards outside. Had he come on his own?

Carter took one look at him and started laughing that irritating nasal guffaw of his. "Please tell me you don't have your guards posted outside like a beacon."

Soren sniffed. "You don't expect me to go places without them, do you?"

Cranston rolled his eyes. "Afraid one of the conservative gun-toters is going to express their displeasure with you?"

Soren thinned his lips. The look on Carter's face said he hoped one would. "Why did you call me here, Cranston?"

The corpulent politician swirled his ice through his whiskey. "Can I pour you a drink?"

Soren cussed him. "No you can't. Just get to the point."

"Testy as ever, I see." Cranston's brows slumped low over his eyes, and he sat up far enough to set his drink on the table before him. "We may have a problem."

"Yeah? What's that?"

"An undercover officer apparently caught wind of our little... project. He was in the warehouse where we met last time and filmed our conversation."

"What!?" Soren swore. "Security was your purview that night."

Cranston patted the air in a calm down gesture. "My guys did their job. They swear no one was in there five minutes before our meeting. So someone had to have leaked information that led the officer to the place and he knew enough to get the job done. But it's all been taken care of. The undercover officer is out of the picture and the evidence has been erased."

"You killed a cop!?"

Cranston gave him a withering look. "I haven't touched anyone. And none of this can be traced back to us. Trust me on that."

"There is no *us,* and don't forget it."

Cranston blew a sound of dismissal. "There was plenty of *us* when we were first approached with this idea."

Soren turned for the stairs. He was done here. But he couldn't resist a parting warning tossed over his shoulder. "If any of this gets out, Cranston, you're a dead man."

Carter Cranston leaned back against the couch, relieved to have the meeting over. He tossed back the remaining whiskey in his glass and released a breath with puffed cheeks. At least Bane hadn't stuck around, because the man terrified him. He was brutal and ruthless and wouldn't hesitate to follow through on the threat he'd just leveled. Wouldn't hesitate for even a blink.

And the truth was, Carter wasn't at all sure that the leak was contained.

The undercover cop was dead, sure. Even the officer who might have seen some of the data on the phone. But there was the slight issue of the girl. The witness who'd spoken to the undercover officer before he died. She seemed to have slipped through their fingers.

One minute his man had been following her and the two detectives through the streets, and the next moment they had ducked into a restaurant. By the time his man had made his way into the dining room, they'd disappeared. And though he'd circled the block searching for them, he hadn't been able to pick up their trail again. He'd reported that neither detective had returned to the station.

Yeah, the girl was a huge risk. They were going to have to find her.

If they didn't, it wouldn't only be Soren threatening his life. The boss was going to be livid.

Speaking of that, it was time to make that call. He shored up his confidence and pulled his phone from inside his coat. This was as private a place as any.

The number rang three times.

"Hello?"

Carter pulled in a breath of confidence. "Boss, there's been a little incident I need to report."

Kate Dollinger paced the small space behind her desk in the front office of the Sheriff's building, flipping back and forth from the picture to the video on her phone. When she heard the helicopter, she glanced out her window to see it flying past on the near horizon.

She squinted. What was that dangling from the belly? Scurrying around her desk, she pressed her face to the window to get a better look. She snatched up the pair of binoculars from where she kept them on the corner of her desk and trained them on the chopper in the distance.

Why in the world would Holden and Jay be flying with the back door of the helicopter open? And why was the descent rope dangling from the belly?

The helicopter disappeared from view behind the tall bank of trees this side of the airport.

Kate plunked her binoculars back on her desk and propped her hands on her hips. Her eyes narrowed. The alarm on her phone chimed and she slapped it off. It was time to leave already. On Thursdays and Fridays she went home at noon to watch her grandson while her daughter went to work.

Well, she would just have to be a little late today. Tapping her phone to her lips, she paced the office for the next fifteen minutes, getting nothing done. Finally, she heard Jay's familiar clunking boots on the office steps.

She leapt to the stack of files she'd strategically set near the filing cabinet to look like she was busy organizing old cases.

Jay gave a start when he stepped through the door. "What are you still doing here?" He hooked his Stetson on the rack by the door. "It's past noon." He hurried by her and she could tell he didn't want to talk.

She decided to let him get away with it this time. "Of course. You're right." She made a show of hurrying into her coat. Better keep the man pacified. "Where's Holden?"

Jay waved a hand. "He'll be along. You have a good afternoon." With that, he disappeared into the bathroom at the back of the office.

She narrowed her eyes.

First, they hadn't let her see what was in that orange bucket, then they'd scurried around making calls that they hadn't let her place and gathering a cooler and ice of all things, and now Jay had returned without Holden and wasn't speaking to her in anything but short chops.

This was probably the first truly important thing that had happened since she'd been hired. And it was crucial that she stay on top of things. And they were blocking her from the information she needed.

Where could the sheriff be?

She headed to her car and fumbled to get her key in the lock. Tonight was sure to be another sleepless night.

Chapter 9

The warmth of the shower helped revive Camryn, and she felt like a new woman by the time she slipped into the clean clothes and headed down the stairs to find the kitchen. The bagginess of the clothes was driving her crazy, and she didn't have on any makeup. But she hadn't been wearing much yesterday either, so it wasn't like her appearance was going to be a shock to the sheriff.

The tantalizing scent of garlic and beef wafted from the kitchen, making it easy to find.

When she stepped into the room, Holden looked up and smiled. "Feeling better?" He took her in from head to toe as he wiggled a basket of french fries in a deep fryer.

She rested her elbows against the bistro-height marble bar on one side of the island. "Yes, thank you. Whatever you are making smells delicious."

"There's not much in this world that a barbecued cheeseburger can't fix."

"Yum!" Her stomach rumbled at the thought.

"It's a bit cold for the back patio, but the dining room has a nice hundred-and-eighty-degree view." He indicated the table which was set into the curve of a prominent bay window.

"I can't imagine there's a room in this house that doesn't have a nice view. Can I help you with anything?"

He shook his head. "The fries are done, I'm just serving them up, then we can eat. I've already set the table. What can I get you to drink?"

"Water is great thanks."

He had been right about the view, she thought, as she sank into her seat. "How do you ever leave this place? I think I might sit right here and never move."

He smiled as he set a plate before her. "I was thinking about that this morning when I saw how amazed you were at the view. I guess, living here, we tend to take the beauty all around us for granted."

"Speaking of taking things for granted, I don't think I've thanked you for your willingness to keep me safe. I'm sure that wasn't on your agenda for the next two weeks."

He waved dismissal. "Glad I could help. It's all part of the job. Speaking of that, let's lay down some ground rules for while you are here. I don't want you leaving the house unless you let me know so that I can go with you. And I'd really prefer that you stayed off the grounds. Too much risk of anyone who happened to be passing by seeing you and wondering what you're doing here."

And just like that her appreciation and gratitude dissipated. The thought of leaving the house hadn't even crossed her mind yet, but the fact that he had told her she couldn't made her want to go exploring. "I thought you said you lived on twenty acres and your neighbors were gone during the day."

He swept a french fry through the pile of ketchup on his plate and held it as he replied, "True. The chances are slim that anyone would see you. But I would like to keep them as slim as possible."

Her irritation mounted. "This is all so ridiculous."

He didn't seem fazed by her perturbation. "There's a library at the end of the hall if you like to read. And the TV in the living room is hooked up to the Internet, so you can stream whatever you like. Make yourself at home in the kitchen if you like to cook. I can get you whatever groceries you might want from town. Look at it as an unexpected vacation." He gave her a smile.

She drew patterns in her ketchup with a french fry. "The problem is, I can't afford a vacation right now." She stuffed the fry into her mouth. Maybe that would keep her quiet. She hadn't meant to blurt out her financial woes.

He snagged the roll of paper towels from the middle of the table and tore one off to use as a napkin. "Actually, if it's work you're looking for, I might have some things that you could help me with. The department has been needing some file organization. I could bring some boxes home on the pretense of working on them myself, but I'll pay you to do it for me."

Her relief at the offer was so sudden and palpable that it brought tears to her eyes. "That would be such a blessing. I am really good at organization. And research. If you need help with research, I can do that too."

Holden tore off another paper towel and handed it to her. "I didn't mean to make you cry."

She dabbed at her eyes. "It's not you. I think I'm simply exhausted, and so much has happened in the last twenty-four hours that my emotions are all over the place."

"Well, as soon as we are done eating you can go up to your room and take a long nap if you want. Did you get any clothes ordered?"

She shook her head. "No. Not yet. I will do that right after lunch. But I was wondering..." She tucked her lower lip between her teeth, unsure how to broach the subject of paying for the clothes. She had always made it a practice not to keep a credit card. She had a debit card, but her bank account was running on fumes until her next check deposited.

He snapped his fingers, seemingly able to read her thoughts. "Right. I need to give you a credit card."

She relaxed a little. "Yes. Thank you."

It didn't take them long to polish off their burgers and fries, and then he rose and took their plates to the sink. "Give me a moment to grab my wallet." He disappeared down the hall.

She took the opportunity to step to the windows to take in the amazing view once more. She didn't see how anyone could get used to such beauty.

He returned and handed her a card. "Buy whatever you need."

"Uh..." She fidgeted a little, feeling helpless at having to ask for every little thing. "I don't seem to have any cell-service out here. Could I get a password to your Wi-Fi so that I could use my phone to place the clothing order? And the address for this place?"

"Of course. Sorry. I should have thought to offer those right off the bat. I can give you the password to the Wi-Fi. But you are more than welcome to use my laptop. That might be easier than trying to order on your phone."

Again, her relief was palpable. "Yes. That would be helpful thank you."

When he showed her to the computer room and she sat at the desk, she glanced at the card and noticed it had his name on it. She offered it back to him. "Did you give me the wrong card?"

He waved a hand. "No, it's the right one. I'll leave you to it." He left before she could say more.

She tapped the card against one palm, considering. Would his expense card have his name on it? It wasn't beyond the realm of possibility. She didn't want to be a charity case. But neither did she want to pester him if this was indeed his office card.

With a sigh, she decided to leave it be. She jiggled the mouse to wake up the computer.

It only took her a few minutes to find some of her favorite brands and place her orders. Her face blazed as she pressed *buy* on several pairings of underthings. She would need to make sure to be the one to open all of the boxes.

She didn't see him in the main part of the house when she was done so she tucked the card into the small zippered pocket of the sweats she was wearing and retreated to her room. Maybe a short nap would help her power through the rest of the day.

She was asleep almost before her head hit the pillow.

Holden woke the next morning with a concern weighing on him. If he was going to stay out here at his place to protect Camryn, he needed to present the office—check that—he needed to present *Kate* with an excuse.

Jay and August, his other deputy, were trustworthy and wouldn't breathe a word of why he was out here, but Kate most definitely would grow curious and start gossiping if he didn't come up with a good reason. And the last thing he wanted was for word to get about town that Camryn was at his place. Everett was just across the water and a little south. There was always someone who knew someone, and word could spread like wildfire—especially when you didn't want it to.

Maybe the fact that he hadn't taken a vacation for the entire time he'd been San Juan's sheriff would suffice? He immediately cast that idea aside. Kate would never believe he was taking a spur-of-the-moment week off.

He could claim to be under the weather. That could work. At least for the first week. After that, he would see where the case was at and figure out another excuse if he needed to. He didn't like the deception, but like Rahab who had lied to save the spies, he felt like this time he could justify it.

He glanced at his watch. Kate wouldn't be in the office yet. She was likely still at Sunkissed Biscuits, the bakery across town, picking up their every-other-day order of apple turnovers and cheese Danishes. He'd give it another ten minutes.

He pulled out one of the packages of bacon he'd purchased from a local butcher shop when he'd bought a whole hog last year. Seeing only three packages left in the freezer reminded him he needed to put in another order.

By the time he heard Camryn coming down the stairs, he had the bacon draining on a paper towel, eggs whisked and waiting in a bowl, and an assorted variety of veggies chopped.

She stepped into the kitchen right as he was reaching for a paper towel to wipe his fingers.

This morning she'd tucked her hair up into a messy bun that appeared to be held in place with a couple pencils. She'd rolled every item of his clothing to get them to fit better. The waist of his sweats was rolled down, while the hems were rolled up and tucked tight. She'd tied a knot in one corner of his jersey, and the effect drew his attention to her slender waist.

The woman was positively stunning.

She gave him a funny little look. "Morning."

Holden was chagrined to note that his hand remained frozen only midway to the roll of paper towels. He snatched one off and concentrated on wiping the green pepper juice from his fingers. "Morning. Hope you slept well." He hadn't seen her since after lunch yesterday.

She wrinkled her nose. "Maybe tonight. I fell asleep early, but then I woke at ten and couldn't seem to catch more than a few minutes each hour after that. I finally gave up around three and have been reading a book I took from the shelf in my room. I hope that was all right."

"Of course." He wadded the paper towel and tossed it in the trash. "It can be hard to relax after a trauma such as you experienced. But I want you to know I'm not going to let anything happen to you. You are safe here with me."

He propped his hands on his hips and searched her face, hoping she believed him. He wanted her to be at ease. But after only a moment he could no longer hold her gaze. He pried at a tile with one toe and prayed he wouldn't be made a liar like last time.

"I'm sure I will be. I still am unconvinced I even need protection. I don't think it was fear that kept me awake. Just... so many thoughts running through my head."

A little warning bell called for his attention. "I hope you will take seriously the reasons why the detectives put you in PC—protective custody. We—they don't do that for trivial things. They wouldn't have asked me to watch you if there wasn't a real threat to you." He took in her wide brown eyes. "I don't say that to frighten you, but to beg you to please take my instructions seriously. He stopped short of telling her what had happened the last time he'd been assigned to protect a woman and she hadn't followed his orders.

She seemed to gather herself as she wrapped her arms about her waist. "I need to call my job and let them know I won't be coming in for a while."

He considered. Could he let her call in? Or was it better for her simply to show up and ask for forgiveness later? That might cost her the job. On the other hand, calling in without notice to tell them she couldn't work for two weeks would also likely cost her the job. It was better to be safe.

Holden shook his head. "Afraid you can't do that. Too much risk of the call being traced. All they'd have to do is pinpoint the call to the island, and then it wouldn't be hard for them to figure out who you are staying with. In fact, have you made any calls since you've been here?"

She shook her head. "No. I have no service."

Thank the Lord for that.

"Good. Don't call anyone. These people, they murdered two cops, and if they were willing to go that far, it means they really, really don't want any loose ends to whatever they are trying to cover up." He hesitated. He didn't want to be harsh, but last time he'd erred on the side of allowing his charge to keep her innocence. He couldn't afford to do that this time. "You could be one of those loose ends. Understand? If they've deemed you a threat, they will be out there looking for you. You can't do anything to help them find you. Got it?"

Her eyes were a bit wide, but at least she was nodding.

"Good. Now what do you like in your omelets?"

Kate Dollinger had just sat down at her desk with her pastry and a cup of coffee when the phone rang. She made quick work of swallowing the bite in her mouth. "San Juan Sheriff's Office, how may I help you?"

"Kate, it's Holden."

She frowned. He sounded truly awful. "You sound sick! Are you alright?"

"That's why I'm calling. I'm not going to be able to come in today. Maybe for the rest of the week."

Her frown deepened. That was odd. The man never called in sick. He was either truly ill, or her instincts had been right yesterday. Something was up. Something they weren't telling her about. "You poor thing! I'll bring you some soup." Then she could see if he was hiding something.

"Thanks. That's kind of you. Will you also bring me a few boxes of the old files that need to be scanned in? I can do that work from home."

"You should rest."

"I will. I promise."

She hung up the phone with a frown. She hadn't expected him to be so open to her bringing him food. Maybe he wasn't hiding anything after all.

She downed the last of her pastry and coffee, then stood. "Jay?"

"Yeah?" he called from his office.

"Holden just called in. He's sick. I'm going to go home and grab some jars of soup to take to him."

"All right."

"Was he sick yesterday?" A thought registered and her brows shot up. "You aren't feeling sick, are you?" Maybe the contents of that orange bucket had made them sick.

She heard Jay rise from his desk and a moment later he stepped into the hall in front of his office. "I feel fine. Holden had to get in the water yesterday to retrieve the bucket. Maybe he caught a cold from that."

Her lips thinned. "Maybe." She wasn't buying it. "What happened yesterday in Everett?"

He shrugged. "An undercover cop was murdered. Holden flew there to talk to a couple detectives about that."

She narrowed her eyes, considering. Could Jay be trusted? "You aren't holding out on me, are you?"

He plunked his hands on his hips. "If there's anything you need to know, I'll let you know."

She huffed. My, but he was feeling high and mighty all the sudden, wasn't he? The kid knew one little thing she didn't know and now he was lording it over her like she was a peasant of old and he was the landowner.

She hefted the stack of three file boxes from the corner. "He asked me to bring these out so he could do some scanning from home."

Jay nodded. "That's fine. August comes on at ten. And I've got the phones if anyone calls." With that, he disappeared back into his office.

Kate grumbled to herself as she loaded the file boxes into her trunk and climbed behind her wheel.

Something was not right. Both Holden and Jay were acting... off. There was definitely something they were hiding.

And she was determined to find out what.

Chapter 10

Camryn was seated on the back patio reading her book, when Holden poked his head out the sliding door. "She's here."

"That was fast." She rose and followed him inside. He'd warned her that the station secretary would be arriving with some food and the files he wanted her to work on. He'd also mentioned that the woman was a bit nosy and would want to see for herself that he was "sick."

"Yeah. Not even I expected her to get here this fast. I thought she'd come around noon."

They stepped into the entry. A flash of movement at the frosted sidelight revealed the shadow of a plump woman.

Camryn froze. "Can she see in here?" she whispered.

Holden shook his head and responded in a voice she could barely hear. "It's too dark in here. We can only see her silhouette because of the bright sunlight."

The doorbell rang.

He touched her elbow. "Up the stairs," he urged her quietly. "I'll come get you when she leaves."

"Wait," she paused one step up. "If you are going to pass off being sick, you need to look the part." The man definitely didn't look ill. She swept him with an assessment. More like a GQ model.

She slid her fingers in his hair and mussed it, only then realizing how close that put her to him.

His intense blue gaze drilled into hers. He propped one arm against the wall and the other against the stair rail, looking like he had all the time in the world.

She hesitated, fingers still entwined in his curls. "Sorry if I'm overstepping," she whispered.

He shook his head. "I'm not complaining. Do I look sicker?" His mouth quirked.

She felt her face heat. No. He definitely didn't. She pinched his cheeks to make them red, doing her best to ignore the feel of his stubble beneath her fingers. "The sickest I can make you look on such short notice."

His focus dipped to her mouth. He swallowed and stepped back. "Next time I'll give you more time." He winked.

Her face flamed as she fled up the stairs.

Holden pondered as he watched Camryn disappear. Had he really winked at her? He knew the risks that came with allowing himself to become attracted to a woman in his custody. He gripped the back of his neck. These thoughts had to stop, and now.

Sure, she was an attractive woman. She was sweet, thoughtful, and totally innocent of the violence that criminals wouldn't hesitate to foist on her.

He gave a definitive nod. He'd have a talk with her. If her blush just now was any indication, she was feeling the chemistry too. But they couldn't let it take over. They were both old enough to handle this.

This was an employment situation. That was all. Employment. Plain and simple.

The doorbell rang again.

He spun toward the door, then cracked it open the barest of inches. He peered through the crack and gave his voice the best gravelly rasp he could summon. "I think you should leave everything on the porch. I'd hate to give you whatever this is."

"Nonsense!" Kate shoved the door with one foot and barreled in, carrying a basket filled with jars. "I'm not afraid of a little old flu bug."

Holden shoved his hands into his hoodie pockets and huddled into his shoulders trying to look cold. He noticed her searching gaze as she led the way to the kitchen. He rolled his eyes. She wasn't here to give him food so much as to see what might be going on out here. He only hoped she'd be satisfied by the time she left. He knew how she liked to chat with her cousin who lived in Everett.

"Did you bring the files?" he asked.

She set the basket on the kitchen island and *tsk*ed, stepping in front of him. Before he could pull back, she had her hand on his forehead.

She frowned. "You don't feel too hot."

He shrugged one shoulder. "Took some Tylenol about an hour ago." The lies were compounding.

"Well, at least that's helping with the fever. Your cheeks are red as strawberries." She set to unpacking jars from the basket. "I'll get the file boxes for you in a minute, but don't you go working too hard when you need to be resting."

"I won't."

She nudged two canning jars together. "These two are homemade beef stew." Another three jars were clumped together. "These are chicken noodle. And these last two are a chicken base that you add dumplings to." She withdrew two bags of a white floury substance from the basket. "That's these. All you have to do is add a cup of milk and one egg. I've written it right here on the baggie, see? Then you drop them on top of the boiling stock and let them cook for ten minutes uncovered, then cover it and cook for another ten minutes." She set the bags on the counter. "It's all in the instructions. Now, let me see what's in your refrigerator. Do you need anything else?" She yanked the door open and began rearranging things all while hemming and hawing under her breath. "Yes, you could definitely use some more vegetables. I'll bring you some. Hank... well, I keep his garden going all year long in the greenhouse, so it's no hardship. Trust me, I have plenty." She snagged the first jars of soup. "I'll put these on the top shelf here."

Holden suddenly noticed the two identical glasses and plates from their breakfast in the sink. Would she notice that both plates still had egg bits on them? He meandered to the sink and took up the first plate, rinsing it beneath the tap. Why hadn't he let Camryn do the dishes when she'd offered.

Thankfully, Kate's focus was still on loading jars into his fridge. He rinsed the second plate and loaded it into the dishwasher after the first.

Kate turned and looked at him. Her gaze bounced from him to the dishes. "I'll do those for you in just a moment." She flapped a hand. "Go lie down on the couch. I'll bring you tea."

He quirked a brow.

"Okay, coffee. You probably don't even have tea around here. I'll put it on the list of things to bring. Nothing helps you feel better like a nice hot cup of tea."

"I'll have to take your word for it." He closed the dishwasher and ambled out of the kitchen. There wasn't anything more incriminating in there. It wouldn't hurt to let her snoop around.

He took to the couch, that would let him see the base of the stairs. He didn't want her getting any ideas about going to the upper level. She puttered and talked to herself in the kitchen.

After a moment she hollered. "Oh, turn on the news. Did you hear about the jailbreak that happened in Everett the other night? Seems there was a guy who got away. He's unaccounted for."

Holden grunted. Of course he had heard, but when he'd left they were still searching for the man, and he'd been so concentrated on keeping Camryn safe that he hadn't looked into it more. No officer of the law liked to hear something like that.

He tugged his phone from his pocket and pulled up the local news site.

Sure enough. His brows shot up when he saw who it was who'd escaped. "Kirk Vossler!" He tapped the link. Vossler actually owned property out here on San Juan. "Kate, did any notification about this come into the office?"

"Yes. Yesterday. That's why I'm telling you!" Dishes and silverware clattered in the dishwasher.

Holden pinched the bridge of his nose. It wouldn't do him a bit of good to chastise her for not telling him sooner.

He needed to call Jay and have him go by the man's estate. It was currently occupied by a caretaker named Jody Horton. They'd had dealings with her on two occasions when petty vandals broke into the property, though not much had been damaged on either occasion. But they needed to keep an eye out for Vossler. He'd been convicted for inciting a riot when it had been proven last year that he'd paid a group of troublemakers to destroy several Everett city blocks. He'd been slated for transport to a more secure facility next week.

He lowered his phone and listened. Kate was still in the kitchen.

He minimized the article and punched Jay's name.

"Hello?"

"Jay, Kate just told me about the jail break. Did she tell you?"

"Jail break?"

"In Everett. Kirk Vossler."

Jay swore.

"Yeah, we need to post a lookout at his place. Any activity we'll need to report. I'm surprised no one has shown up at the station already to let us know they'll be watching his place." The last sentence was half statement, half question.

"No one has shown up here. At least not while I was on duty."

"Just a sec." Holden lowered the phone again. "Hey, Kate!" He jolted. She was standing in the living room archway. "Hey. No one stopped by the office to say they'd be staking out the Vossler place, did they?"

"No." She stepped forward with a cup of coffee on a tray and bent to set it on the coffee table. "Would you like cream in your coffee?"

His irritation with her lingering mounted, but then he had a pang of conscience. It was probably hard on her to live alone. Her husband had died only a few months ago. It probably felt good for her to be able to take care of someone other than herself.

Still, he couldn't forget her propensity to gossip.

"Just black. Thanks."

He waited till she'd left the room before he resumed his conversation with Jay. "You and August figure out a rotating schedule. Put me on four to midnight. I hate to leave—well, you know—but you two can't cover the place twenty-four seven on your own."

"We could each take nine hours. That would leave you with six. You could be home by ten that way."

Holden pondered. It wasn't really fair to ask his deputies to take longer shifts, but in this case, he had Camryn's safety to think of. "Yeah, if you two don't mind. That would be better. And…" He double-checked the door, thankful to find it empty. "Maybe you wouldn't mind crashing here during my shift?"

Jay hesitated for only a moment. "You got it, boss."

"Thanks." He hung up the phone and released a breath. That eased his mind about leaving Camryn here alone.

Kate continued to fiddle with a little of this and a little of that, but thankfully she never approached the stairs.

Almost thirty minutes later she puffed into the living room carrying three filing boxes. "These are the last of the files from 1999 that we haven't gotten scanned into the computer yet. Where should I put them?"

"There by the desk is fine." He pointed into the den that opened off the living room with double French doors.

She set them down and gave him a pointed look. "Promise me you won't work too hard."

He gave her a smile that surprisingly he meant. "Thanks for caring, Kate. I promise to rest as much as I can."

"Well, all right then." She dug for her car keys in her purse. "I'll leave you be, but I'll be back tomorrow with some fresh veggies and some baked goods. I didn't see one cookie in your entire kitchen."

She had gone through his cupboards? Truth was, he got so many carbs at the office that he tried really hard not to keep many around the house. But maybe Camryn would like some cookies. "Thanks, Kate."

"You bet. I'll let myself out." She left then, but he held his breath until he heard her tires crunching over the gravel as she pulled away from the property. He'd half expected her to pop back in to mention something she'd forgotten.

Chapter 11

Camryn sat quietly on her bed, reading, afraid to move lest a floorboard creak and alert the woman downstairs. For a while she could hear her clattering dishes in the kitchen—at least she presumed it was her. But then the house turned silent.

She held her breath, listening. Had the woman left? Was it safe to move now? From her room in the back of the house she hadn't heard any vehicles. She'd better remain still until Holden came for her since they hadn't laid out a plan of what they would do after the woman left.

She tried to concentrate on her book, but it was no use. She set it down, leaned her head against the headboard, and took in the gorgeous island-and-evergreen-mottled ocean view out her window. Today it was cloaked in a misty shroud. If she had to be in protective custody and continue worrying about how she was going to make next month's payments, this place certainly gave her nothing to complain about. Certainly, if things were different it wouldn't hurt her feelings at all to live in a place like this. Not to mention enjoying the company that came with it.

Her face heated.

She'd better remember that the handsome sheriff downstairs would never be interested in a relationship with a going-nowhere-fast woman like her.

She sighed. In college she'd had big plans. Plans to become a teacher. Invest in the lives of children. She'd intended to find Mr. Right too—with God's help, of course. A man who would sweep her off her feet and protect her when she needed it, but mostly give her the courage to stand up for herself. Most important of all, he would support her dream of teaching and give her three children of her own—all born at the beginning of the summer so she wouldn't have to take time off from work. She should have had two of those children by now, according to the plan she'd jotted in her journal during her senior year in high school.

She shook her head. How naïve she'd been.

Her mother would have said, "God had other plans."

Camryn gripped the back of her neck and watched the ferry that looked like a toy from this distance as it sailed north through a gray mist. She just wasn't sure that God took the time to care about such things. She'd read one time that God had sort of set the world spinning and then stepped back to watch. After the year she'd had, she felt like that could totally be true. It certainly felt like it was true.

Yet, if that were the case, why had He come down to earth to die for the sins of mankind?

She blew out a breath and pushed such weighty thoughts to the back of her mind.

Whatever the right answer was, Mr. Right had never materialized during college. A few had looked promising at first. But they'd turned out to be Mr. Only-Living-For-Himself, Mr. Stuck-Up, and Mr. Mouse.

Then had come graduation and the job hunt. Her hunt through the large Seattle metropolis, hadn't offered any "real" teaching positions. Her only offers had been for assistant positions, one of which she'd been working until the world melted down at the beginning of the year.

And now it looked like even the job she'd found waiting tables might be in jeopardy because she'd been in the proverbial wrong place at the wrong time.

Despite all that, she'd been kept safe. Detective Lexington had arrived at the exact right moment, it seemed. Because though he hadn't been willing to address it with her, she could tell that he hadn't trusted that other officer—the one with the cold eyes that still sent shivers up and down her spine. Perhaps God had used Detective Lexington, and now Sheriff Parker, to protect her.

Tears pricked her eyes, and she gave in to the persistent nudge she'd felt over the last few days to pray. "God, what are You doing to me? I just can't seem to get ahead. Have You heard any of my prayers over the past year? I mean I know You technically hear them. But do You care? Do You care that Mom passed, leaving me alone in the world? Do You care about the financial stresses I'm under? Because it doesn't really feel like You do. I've been asking You to help me, not bring me out to the middle of the boonies, even if they are beautiful, while my finances crumble around me—again."

A verse that she'd memorized as a girl whispered through her memory. *But seek first his kingdom and his righteousness, and all these things will be given to you as well. Therefore do not worry about tomorrow, for tomorrow will worry about itself. Each day has enough trouble of its own.*

She shivered. Her tears spilled over. For months she'd been worried about nothing but her own personal well-being. She'd been working so much she hadn't often made it to church like she should. She certainly hadn't been seeking God's kingdom or His righteousness.

Maybe bringing her out here to the middle of nowhere was what it had taken for God to get through to her.

"Oh God, forgive me," she whispered.

A tapping sounded on her door. "Camryn? You can come out now. If you come down, I'll show you the files I need you to scan. And something's come up that I need to tell you about."

"Coming." She dashed at her tears and stepped to the door. At least she was going to get a little income for helping while she was here in hiding. Maybe that was God's answer, though she couldn't see how scanning a few files was going to pay enough to cover her school loans and her rent for next month.

She gave herself a mental shake. Would she ever learn to count her blessings instead of focusing on the negative?

She opened the door.

Holden, who had started to turn away, paused and gave her a look. He adjusted his stance to face her fully. "You okay?"

"What? Yes, I'm fine."

He reached up to touch her cheek, and when he pulled his hand back, his fingers glistened with moisture. "This would say otherwise. Want to talk about it?" He rubbed his fingers together.

She waved a hand. "It's nothing. I'll be fine, honest."

"Uh-huh." His steady scrutiny never left her face. Nor did he budge. And he was blocking her exit from the room. "I know this isn't easy. You've been a real trooper. So much so, I almost forgot how distressing all this must be for you."

Despite her best wishes, she felt tears welling up again. She forced a laugh and pressed her fingers beneath her eyes. "I'm fine, really. I just... I was praying and God..." She wasn't sure how to complete the thought. It wasn't like God had spoken to her, yet wasn't that the biggest way God spoke—through His Word? Finally feeling reassured that God loved her and did truly care for her should fill her with elation. Yet, more tears welled.

"Hey. Come here." Holden touched her arm and urged her closer.

Before she realized what she was doing, she'd settled into the comfort of his embrace and nestled her head beneath his chin. His aftershave, a mixture of pine and spice, tantalized her senses, eliciting pictures of sturdy mountain evergreens. And the warmth of his arms settled around her like a comforting blanket on a cold day.

Without her permission, her shoulders began to shake and sobs wracked her. "I...don't...even...know why...I'm crying," she managed between gasps for breath.

He stroked one hand up and down her back and settled his chin against her head. "You've had quite a shock. Seeing someone killed is never something you can prepare yourself for."

She relaxed against him, appreciating the comfort of his embrace. It seemed to calm her deep inside. Soothe the raw, agitated edges of her soul. She took a steadying breath. Wiped at another stream of tears. Was finally able to gather herself.

Were her tears really because of seeing that man die? If she were honest, she hadn't thought of him much in the past hours. She'd been more stressed and concerned with her own financial woes. Had she pushed the thoughts of his death away because of selfishness? Or a lack of capacity to deal with what she'd witnessed on that Everett street?

"I wish I could have saved him. I tried but he was just so...broken after that car—" The dam holding back her tears burst again.

"Come on. Can you walk?" Holden took her hand and urged her to follow him down the stairs. He led her into the living room and settled onto the couch, tugging her down beside him. She missed the comfort of his embrace. Of his hand around hers. But he didn't offer them again. Instead he said, "I'll get you some... Well, coffee's probably not the thing. I'll bring warm milk."

He left the room before she could gather herself enough to reply.

Yesterday, Mount Baker and the west coast shoreline had hovered in the distance. But today the vista's only boast was a sheet of gray. And a fine sleet had started to fall. The two islands across the way that had been green when she arrived were now coated with a dusting of white. The flagstones on the patio also sported a new skiff of sloppy snow.

The scene made her cold just to look at it. She tugged a throw from the end of the couch and swung it around her shoulders.

Holden returned a few minutes later with two steaming mugs.

His held coffee, she noted with a touch of jealousy as he sank back down beside her and handed her the other cup. He settled into the corner of the couch angling toward her and stretching one arm along the back. He gave a nod toward her cup. "Try it."

She wrapped her hands around the warmth and inhaled a spicy sweet aroma. She cautiously tasted the frothy drink. "Mmmm."

Holden smiled. "Warm milk is always better with a little sugar, cinnamon, and nutmeg. I stopped short of adding the egg that would make it eggnog."

Still huddled in her blanket, she glanced over at him. "I'm sorry I fell apart on you."

His gaze was serious when he asked, "Do you believe in God, Camryn?"

She felt her jaw go a little slack at that. It was almost as if he'd been eavesdropping on the thoughts she'd been having upstairs. "I do believe in God."

"What do you mean by that?"

This time she truly was taken aback. "What?"

He pondered for a moment, watching the sleet coming down outside. "I mean, do you believe in God as a concept? Just some mythos out in the universe somewhere? Or do you believe He's a relational being who wants to fellowship with us?"

Camryn tucked her feet under herself. "I grew up in church, and I know I'm supposed to say He wants a relationship, but I confess I've been having doubts lately. Not about His existence, but about whether He really cares about the little everyday things, you know?" She held her breath, halfway waiting for him to scoff at her unbelief. "But just now, upstairs, I was praying and... I don't know. A verse came to mind, and it really felt like God was taking time to talk directly to me."

He nodded and transferred his gaze to her once more. "There's a story in the Bible about a man who came to Jesus. He wanted a miracle for his son. He said to Jesus 'If You can, please help us.' And Jesus replied, 'If I can? Everything is possible for those who believe.' The man immediately exclaimed, 'I do believe. Help my unbelief!'" Holden leaned forward and set his coffee cup on the table before settling in his corner of the couch again. "That has been my prayer for several years, off and on. Sometimes I find believing easier. But in the times when I'm struggling, I pray that He'll help my unbelief, because I know"—he tapped his temple—"despite what I feel"—he tapped his heart—"that belief is what I need in order to have a relationship with God that's on the right foundation." He stood then, lifted his cup, and squeezed her shoulder before walking from the room.

Camryn searched through their conversation as she took another sip of the delicious drink. She nestled into the corner of the couch and closed her eyes. *Thank you, Lord. Please do help my unbelief.*

Kirk Vossler rose from the laptop and pressed thumb and forefinger to his eyes. There was one thing about being in a cell for the last couple months—he'd forgotten the strain a long day working on a computer put on his eyes.

He flicked aside the faded yellow curtain on his motel room window. He cursed the winter chill and strode over to bump the old thermostat north a couple degrees. He'd been stuck in this tiny room for too long. And the temperature never seemed to be right. Too hot one moment, so he would bump the heat down. But then within a couple hours the room would be freezing cold again.

It irritated.

Yet he couldn't leave yet.

He'd already almost been caught as it was, thanks to the incompetence of his men.

The murder of that undercover cop was not supposed to have happened a couple blocks from the jail where he was breaking out. They were supposed to pull that job on the north end of town so most of the units would be far from the jail. Their thin excuses that Treyvon refused to get in the vehicle with them and then bolted before they could grab him hadn't strengthened his confidence in them.

He hoped they were going to pull off the next steps of the plan with more accuracy.

He glanced toward his computer. Everything on his end was almost in place. He had a few more hours of work, and then everything would be a go.

For the first time in several days, he smiled. The money was all in place and ready to be put to work.

By the end of the week he would be on his way to becoming not just rich, but filthy rich. And several others—carefully selected contacts from many sectors of society—were slated to benefit financially as well.

This was all thanks to the ingenuity of his first love. God bless her. She was a gift he hadn't known he needed. When this was all over, he owed her a trip to Greece. In fact, maybe they'd move there for a while. At least until he could forge, backdate, and solidify a new identity.

With a grunt, he sank back down in front of his computer. For now, he had more work to do.

Chapter 12

Damien stopped by Case's desk. "The lab is done analyzing the street-cam footage from the other night. Camryn was pretty accurate with her description. We got a plate from the car. It's registered to a Malcom McDonalds."

Case's lips thinned. "We taking bets on the fact that's an alias?"

"Highly probable."

"That we're taking bets? Or that it's an alias?"

Damien grinned. "Come on. Warrant has been served. I've got the address. Ed and Gray are coming with us, along with several other units."

Case stood, grabbed his suit coat, and followed him to the door.

The address was in a low-rent neighborhood where the houses were crammed together cheek-by-jowl and most of the lawns were overgrown. House after house sported dead shrubbery and empty flowerbeds, and many had boarded up windows.

The address was claimed by a faded yellow rambler on the corner of Fifteenth and Cedar.

Damien double-checked the plates. "That's our vehicle." He swung a finger to Ed and Gray in the vehicle behind them to take the rear of the place. Two marked cars also pulled up across the street.

The kit-lifted car sat in the driveway—a dark blue Pontiac GTO with original rims and near-perfect chrome.

Damien whistled. "That's a beaut!"

"Expired tabs," Case said.

"Have you no shame? At least take a moment to admire the lines of such a classic."

Case tilted his head. "Can we get back to work now?"

Damien sighed. "Fine."

They left their vehicle at the curb and circled the car. Sure enough, there was a good-sized dent in the front fender.

Damien looked at Case. "They didn't even bother to conceal it?"

Case shrugged a shoulder. "Let's face it. Anyone who runs a cop down on a monitored street is already a few bricks short of a full load."

"True, I guess. But this just seems...too overt."

"Maybe."

The curtain flicked at the window. "Pigs!" someone shouted from inside the house.

Damien pulled his gun. "Let's go!"

They heard the backdoor of the house crash open, and a dog barked raucously.

"Freeze!"

"Get on the ground!"

"Don't shoot, bro. Don't shoot!"

Leaving two officers to watch the front of the house, Damien and Case circled around back. With two uniformed officers and Gray standing by, Ed had a large man on the ground, just outside the rickety fence. He was already cuffing the man's hands behind his back.

"Did anyone else come out?" Case asked.

Gray shook his head. "Not that I saw."

"Get him up. What's your name, man?"

The perp only glowered, refusing to answer.

"Get his ID. We'll go inside." Damien motioned for Case to follow him to the front.

At their knock, a trembling woman in a bright red housecoat answered the door. She stood partially blocking their entrance.

"Ma'am, we are looking for Malcom McDonalds. We have a search warrant for this place. Back away from the door and sit down." Damien held up the warrant for her to see.

The woman complied, saying, "That's him. You done grabbed him already. Ain't nobody else here but me."

A thorough search of the place proved her statement to be true.

The whole time they searched her house, the woman kept repeating that her man had done nothing wrong.

Damien stopped before her. "What's your name?"

"Tatianna."

"Okay, Tatianna. If he's done nothing wrong, why did he run from us?"

She looked down. "He got a parking ticket that we ain't been able to pay. We thought you's here 'bout that."

"I see. So you didn't think we were here about the big dent in the front of your car? The dent that happened when your husband ran down a cop in cold-blooded murder?"

The woman's eyes widened. "No sir! Malcom's a good man. He'd never do such! He done lent the car to a friend, and when we gots it back, it had that dent."

Damien pressed his lips together and looked over at Case.

Case lifted a hand in a gesture that said, "it could be true."

"Who was this friend?" Damien asked her.

"Gandry Wright. They went through school together, but Gandry... He's a banger. I done tol' Malcom it weren't a good idea to let him borrow the car, but he don't never listen to me."

"You know where Gandry lives?"

The woman lowered her gaze to the floor.

"Ma'am?"

"He been stayin' here. But he's at work right now."

"Where does this Gandry work?"

"At the shipment warehouse down near the airport."

"I'll call it in," Case said. "We'll take both men to the station and figure out the truth from there."

Miller had been monitoring the radios all day, and when the call came in for the arrest of Gandry Wright, he knew the time had come to play his part.

He batted Kingston on the arm. "We're right down the street from there. Call it in."

Kingston keyed the mic and reported that they were on their way.

Several other units also responded, and Miller felt his pulse climb. They had to be the first on scene, or this wasn't going to play out how the boss wanted. Not at all.

And he needed that money.

Gandry knew he was in trouble the moment he looked up from his semi-isolated sorting station and saw Miller, grim-lipped and determined, striding toward him.

He thrust his hands into the air. "Don't shoot me, man! Don't shoot!"

"He's got a gun!" Miller shouted, already drawing his weapon.

"No! I—"

Two bullets took him center-chest.

He collapsed to the ground, the package in his hand tumbling away. He could hear several of his co-workers' footsteps running his way as Miller squatted beside him.

Blocking the view from anyone else, Miller pressed a gun into Gandry's hand, wrapping his fingers firmly around the grip. "Sorry man. Boss's orders. Just playing my part."

Gandry tried to speak. But he suddenly couldn't get any breath.

The world went black.

Back at the station, Damien turned off his radio and stepped into the interrogation room. He spent fifteen minutes questioning Malcom McDonalds while Case went down to tech to see what more they may have found with video analysis from street-cams and to check on Malcom's alibi.

Malcom was reticent to speak, and Damien got nothing useful from him, but by the time he was done with the questioning, Damien actually believed his story. Gandry had told Malcom that he'd accidentally gunned the car in first gear instead of reverse as he was pulling from a parking spot and had dented the bumper on a tree.

"And you believed him?"

Malcom fiddled with the cuffs keeping his hands chained to the table. "Not really, man. But I didn't think he'd run over a cop with it! I would have reported that."

Damien sighed. The man sounded sincere.

"All right. I'll be back in a few minutes."

Ed and Gray were waiting for him with the news about Gandry Wright the moment he stepped from the interrogation room.

Across the room, Damien slapped a folder onto Case's desk and leaned onto his palms. "Miller shot him? Right there in the warehouse?"

"He says the guy had a gun." Case scooped his hands back through his hair.

"Seriously?"

Case shrugged.

"Kingston backing him up?"

"Yeah."

Damien sighed. "Can't anything go right with this one?"

"Doubt it. I guess we pray he lives."

"Wait. He's alive?"

Case nodded. "They took him to Providence Medical Center. He's in surgery now."

"That's something, I guess. I know someone who works there. I'll shoot her a text."

"Her, huh?" There was a definite note of teasing in his partner's tone.

Damien let it slide. "We got any footage of the warehouse?"

"I've put in a request for what they've got, but I'm not holding my breath." Case tapped the screen of his iPad on his desk. "I checked Malcom McDonalds' alibi. It's solid. He's on video in a bar clear across town. He couldn't have been anywhere near the scene of the hit-and-run. But guess what we also found?"

Damien quirked a brow.

"Gandry Wright. He walks out of the parking garage just after Treyvon is hit." Case spun the iPad to show him a still.

"So he wasn't the one driving the car?"

"Nope. But get this. He's on video getting *into* the GTO a few minutes later down at Rucker and Pacific."

"That's only a few blocks from the scene."

Case nodded. "The angle's bad, however, and we can't see who the driver is. But the car then drives around to the back of the alley between the Everpark garage and the bank."

"The same alley where Skelly was last seen."

"Yes. Then a few minutes later, it pulls away and heads in the direction of the marina."

"So we analyze the trunk for blood."

"Already got the team on it. There's more."

Damien leaned into his heels and folded his arms, waiting.

"Miller followed Skelly into that alley."

Damien's pulse skipped a beat. "If we can get any footage of today's shooting from the warehouse, that, combined with this, might just be the evidence we've been looking for to prove Miller's dirty."

"My thoughts exactly. I already told Cap we wanted to talk to him. He said we should come in"—he checked the time—"thirty minutes."

Damien nodded. "I'll be ready. Meanwhile, I'll message Sheila and ask her to let us know the minute Wright can speak to us."

"Sheila? Wait a minute." He leaned forward, lowering his voice. "She's not that woman from that abuse case we investigated last year, is she?"

Damien hesitated for only a moment before deciding to skirt the question. "She's a nurse in the ICU."

"Uh-huh." Case had obviously seen right through his dodge.

He pulled up her contact in his phone and tapped to call her.

"Best tread carefully, man. Something like that could cost you your badge." Case eyed him. "How are things going with her?"

"Slow." He waved a hand. "But I'm fine with that." He lifted the phone. "It's ringing."

Case nodded. "Catch you in a few."

Jay Powers' hand trembled as he pressed the phone tighter to his ear. He ought to have known this day was coming, but still, the shock of the request rocked him back a step. "Kill her? Kill who?"

"You know very well who."

He did, but he wasn't about to let on. "I have no idea what you are talking about."

"Careful, Jay." The sound of tires popping over gravel filtered through the connection. "If you refuse to follow orders, you're in danger of being eliminated."

Jay pinched the bridge of his nose. "I've followed all your orders to this point, haven't I?"

"Just don't get cocky." The phone went dead.

Jay propped his hands against his knees and took in several big breaths, blowing them out through pursed lips. This was starting to get real. He was going to have to pick a side.

Before four that afternoon, Camryn stood at the computer in the den off the living room, scanning in old case files. She was thankful for the generous hourly amount Holden had offered for the job. Depending on how long it took her to get everything done, she might be able to pay all her bills next month. Of course, she didn't plan to doddle to get more money, but it was a big relief off her mind to have some income.

She glanced through the French doors that separated the den from the living room. Holden sat on the couch with files from the case that Detectives Lexington and Packard had asked him to review spread over the coffee table. He had a deep furrow between his brows and rubbed one finger against his chin as he read.

Camryn tucked away a grin. He was even more handsome while he was deep in thought than he was when he was smiling at her, and that was saying something. She sighed. She really needed to stop thinking along those lines.

She appreciated that, though she'd fallen apart a bit this morning, he seemed to have taken it in stride without looking down on her. He'd actually gone out of his way to be encouraging in a platonic way.

If she were honest with herself, Holden's earlier aloofness had hurt a little. She did appreciate that he was only performing a job of keeping her safe. And she totally understood that just because he was the first man to capture her interest in years, it didn't mean now was a good time to pursue a relationship. But honestly, would it hurt the guy to at least give her a lingering look once in a while?

She blew at a piece of hair dangling in her eyes. Maybe she simply wasn't his type. Pity.

She rolled her eyes at herself as she slapped another set of pages into the scanner. She'd been commiserating with herself all day.

The doorbell rang. She shot Holden a wide-eyed look. Did she need to scramble upstairs?

He held up one hand, motioning for her to stay where she was. "I think it's Jay getting here to stay with you. I have to go sit on a stakeout for a few hours."

Right. He'd told her about the rich guy who escaped jail.

"Stay there while I see if it's him."

She stood quietly in the doorway of the den, watching him stride into the entry. She could see the door from her position. He looked through the peephole and then jerked his head back and looked her way.

Her heart gave a jolt. Who could it be?

He put his fingers to his lips and motioned for her to go back into the den as he placed his hand on the doorknob.

As he opened the front door, she retreated and glanced around the room for a hiding place.

"Kate. Hi. This isn't a good time. I was about to leave for my shift at the stakeout of the Vossler mansion."

"I won't be a moment." The gravelly feminine voice sounded determined. Heels clicked across the entryway tiles. "I brought you some more food. Should you be going on a stakeout if you're still sick?"

The end of the sentence trailed away as the woman thankfully headed toward the other end of the house, likely to deposit more food in the kitchen.

Camryn eyed the curtains, could she hide there?

No. Too sheer.

A bookshelf offered no hiding spot. The fireplace was also out. The bookshelf on the opposite wall had two lower cupboard doors.

She tiptoed across the room and opened the doors. To her horror, the hinges squealed loudly. And the shelves inside were narrow and filled with old photo albums. No room to hide.

"What was that?" she heard the woman say from beyond the other room. "Did you hear something?"

Camryn winced and left the cupboard open. The last place that offered even a semblance of a hiding place was the open space beneath the desk. However, it wasn't an executive desk. It didn't have a nice dark cubbyhole to crawl into. It did have solid sidewalls and was pushed against one wall, but anyone who stepped into the room and looked down would see her.

It was her only option, however.

"Kate, listen. I really need to get going. You need to leave."

"One moment. I'm telling you I heard something."

Camryn heard footsteps padding across the living room carpet. She dove for the space beneath the desk and hugged her knees to her chest.

The footsteps stopped on the threshold of the room.

Camryn held her breath. If the woman took two more steps, she would be visible.

"See," Holden said. "No one in here. Thanks for the food. I hate to rush you, but the guys are pulling long shifts and I don't want to be late relieving August."

The woman sighed. "I was certain I heard something."

Camryn sank against the sidewall of the desk, blowing out a quiet breath. Yet, she felt a little silly, hiding beneath a desk. This woman couldn't be a danger, could she? She worked for the police department, after all.

That was when the doorbell rang.

Her eyes shot wide. That would be Jay! How would Holden explain his presence here?

The door opened.

"Hey boss, I'm here to relieve..." Jay's words trailed off.

"Why Jay! Imagine meeting you here." Kate's silky words somehow didn't ring true. "To relieve Holden of what?"

A long pause ensued, and Camryn could imagine the two men looking at each other and trying to decide what to do.

She rolled her eyes. This was ridiculous. This busybody needed to be put in her place. Camryn crawled from beneath the desk, but stayed where she was, hidden from view of the entryway.

"There is someone here, isn't there?" Kate's tone was accusatory. "I've known something was amiss ever since Jay flew back to the airport with the rappelling rope dangling. And Jay wouldn't be here if you didn't need him to watch over someone while you're gone. I'm hurt that you haven't trusted me. Why, I could be helping!"

Even from this distance, Camryn could hear the breath that Holden released. "Kate, listen, whatever you think—"

Camryn stepped into the doorway. Three pairs of eyes focused on her from the entryway.

Holden's eyes fell closed.

Jay gripped the back of his neck and studied the floor at his feet.

Kate was older with salt-and-pepper hair that curled over her head like a sleep cap. She gave Camryn a sympathetic look and tilted her head to one side. "Aw! Look at you! You poor dear." The woman rushed at her like a mother hen, arms wide. "Come here." She pulled Camryn into a firm embrace, then set her at arms' length. "Now tell me why you are here."

Camryn shot Holden a look. Did she dare answer? She was second-guessing her boldness of stepping into view.

To her surprise, Holden stepped to her side and wrapped an arm around her shoulders, drawing her close. "Kate, I wanted more time to keep this relationship quiet while we got to know each other, but you're too attentive." He grinned. "I'd like you to meet Camryn. We're...seeing each other."

Kate's brows lifted. She glanced between them, then settled her gaze on Holden. "Sorry. Not buying it. She's the witness from that case over in Everett, isn't she?"

Holden dropped his arm from around her shoulders, and Camryn folded her arms against the chill that suddenly enveloped her.

Holden narrowed his eyes. "How do you know about that?"

Kate shrugged. "I have my sources."

Holden took a step toward her. "Kate. If you breathe a word of this to anyone, it could cost Camryn her life. And it will certainly cost you your job. Understand?"

Kate pulled a face. "There you go again, not trusting me. I wouldn't dare say a word to anyone. Why would you even think so?" She shot Jay a narrow-eyed look, then motioned to Holden. "We'd better get out of here so you can go relieve August." Her focus turned to Camryn then, all smiles as she said, "Hon, I'm sure you are starving out here for some real food. I'll do some grocery shopping and bring a few things by tomorrow. Oh and..." She stepped onto the porch and when she returned a second later, she thrust a stack of boxes at Camryn. "Here are your packages. I saw the delivery drone dropping them off a bit ago."

Camryn could almost imagine the elderly lady hiding out in the bushes with a pair of binoculars.

She cast a guilty look at Holden. She hadn't thought to change her name on the label. Only the address.

Binoculars or not, the woman probably *had* been watching the place out of curiosity, and when she'd seen the drone dropping the packages, had looked at them for the same reason. With Camryn's name on the label, Kate would have known she was here before she stepped through the door today.

Holden pressed his lips together and touched Kate's shoulder. "Remind me to talk to you about detective training. Let's go. I'm already late."

Kate grinned like the Cheshire Cat and then waggled her fingers in a toodle-oo gesture as she stepped through the door in front of Holden.

Chapter 13

Damien folded his arms and stared at the captain, hardly able to believe what he was hearing. "What do you mean it's not enough evidence? Surely we have enough to question Miller and his partner! If only because he shot one of the key perps in our case! Both Gandry Wright and Miller were in the same alley as Skelly right around the time he was killed."

The captain shook his head. "I know it looks bad. But I'm telling you it's too thin. There's no camera at the back end of that alley to prove what time or even *if* that GTO may have pulled in there. You need more."

That was ridiculous. They had film of the GTO turning onto the street that connected to the back end of the alley. And no film of it on the next block past the alley. Just because they couldn't prove the GTO pulled into the alley didn't mean it wasn't ninety-nine percent likely.

A glance at Case showed him gripping his neck and staring out the window toward the city, shoulders stiff. Damien knew him well enough to know that he was working hard to control his irritation with their boss.

The captain stood from behind his desk. "Hate to cut this short, but I have that peaceful protest that's scheduled for downtown tomorrow morning. I need to get to a meeting with the mayor. You boys can see yourselves out." He lifted his jacket from his chair and left the room.

Case spun away from the window and pierced Damien with a look.

There was no need for words.

Both of them were thinking the same thing, and Damien knew it. This cover-up in the force went deep. But as deep as the captain? They'd both worked with the man for over ten years, and he'd never once given them cause to think that he might be on the take.

Until today.

Camryn took her boxes upstairs. Finally, she would have some new things to change into. She couldn't wait to dig into the boxes to see which of her purchases had arrived, but it felt rude to leave Jay downstairs all alone. So she left the packages on her bed and returned to the living room.

He was seated on the couch, scanning the files that Holden had left there, but when she came in, he sat back and draped one arm along the arm of the couch. "Sorry about Kate. She's never one to let a good mystery go to waste." His lips quirked.

Camryn waved a hand. "It's a relief, actually. All this cloak and dagger seems a bit extreme." She wanted to ask him what the look Kate had given him was about but decided she'd better leave well enough alone.

Jay dipped his chin and peered at her. "You never can tell who might be working for the wrong team. Just continue to be careful."

There was something about the way he spoke the warning that made a shiver run down her spine. She folded her arms. "You sound like Holden."

He smiled. "He's trained me well."

She forced herself to smile in return, willing away her unease. It was simply because Holden made her feel so safe, she decided. His presence filled the room and enveloped her with comfort. She pointed a finger toward the kitchen. "I was ready to knock off for the day and start cooking some dinner. I'm sure you know your way around this place better than I do. I'll be in the kitchen.

Dinner should be ready in about an hour." Maybe if she left him here to study the files, she'd be able to settle her jitters.

"Do you mind if I come help?" He rose from the sofa. "I'm pretty good in the kitchen."

So much for escaping him. "N-no. Not at all." Lies. But what else was she to say?

Fine. She would concentrate on cooking and forget that Holden believed someone might be out to kill her. Besides, he wouldn't leave her with someone he didn't trust implicitly. That eased a measure of her tension.

She strode to the fridge and pulled it open. She'd planned to fry up some chicken breasts she'd pulled from the freezer earlier and then create a Cobb salad. Holden had said he wasn't hungry yet and that he'd eat when he got home. The man probably often put work before a meal.

She glanced at Jay as she pulled ingredients from the fridge. "Do you want to fry? Or chop?"

He hesitated as though really weighing the benefit of one over the other. Then he said, "I'll take chopping. Less chance of burning the house down that way."

She quirked a brow. "I thought you said you were good in the kitchen?"

He shrugged. "I may have slightly"—he stretched his arms as wide as they could go—"exaggerated."

With a chuckle, she pulled the chef knife from the block and handed it to him, handle first. "Well, Cobb salads are really easy. I already boiled and peeled the eggs. They only need to be cut in half. Leave a couple, and I'll slice them for Holden when he gets back. They are better when they are freshly cut. At least I think so."

"Gotcha." Jay tugged the cling wrap from the bowl of eggs.

She chatted as she added oil to a frying pan and then transferred the chicken into the pan. "There's also tomatoes, avocados, mushrooms, onions, and some blue cheese. As soon as I get these frying, I'll help you."

She turned to rinse her hands in the sink and yelped. Jay was standing right behind her with the knife held before him.

Hands still held so as not to drip, her gaze shot to his.

He stepped back. "Sorry about that." He motioned past her. "I was coming for the cutting board."

Her heart started beating again. For a moment, it had looked like he intended to stab her. She angled her elbow toward the kitchen island. "There's one right there."

"Thanks. That will be perfect."

He hadn't seen it? Camryn's hands trembled as she soaped and washed them beneath warm water, keeping half an eye on Jay at the island. He seemed intent on slicing the eggs in perfect halves.

She drew in a steadying breath. All this hiding was making her crazy. She needed to turn her thoughts to something else. "So tell me about your childhood. Where did you grow up?" She reached for the towel.

"Right here on the island." He pointed with the knife. "Just down the street, in fact. My parents and Holden's grandparents were neighbors. They were the old money on this island."

"Oh, how nice. Were they friends?"

He nodded. "They were. But my parents were a little younger. They weren't my biological parents actually. They adopted me when I was nine, after my birth mother chose her alcohol over me." There was a bitter edge to the words.

"I'm sorry. That must have been hard." She flipped the chicken and sprinkled it with seasoning.

Behind her, Jay's knife clanged onto the marble of the kitchen island.

She jumped a little at the loud sound but didn't allow herself to look at him. She willed herself to breathe. Constantly being on edge was going to give her heartburn if she wasn't careful. "Your biological father wasn't in the picture?" She turned to rinse her hands of a few oil splatters.

"Not at that time." He offered the clipped words as he carefully sliced two avocados in half.

Sensing that he wasn't comfortable with this conversation she tried to ease her way out of it. "So are your adoptive parents still living?"

"No."

"Oh. I'm sorry." Now what?

He looked up. "Sorry. I realize I sound..." He waved a hand. "I just miss my parents. Being alone isn't easy."

Boy, did she understand that feeling. She was tempted to skirt the subject, but with her own parents' passing, she found catharsis when people asked her about them. She always hated the start of the conversation, but by the end she relished the memories elicited and enjoyed the chance to reminisce about the wonderful people they were. So she pressed ahead. "I've lost both my parents, so I understand that feeling well. How did your parents pass?"

Jay ran the tip of the knife through the flesh of the avocado cupped in his hand. She didn't think she'd ever seen such diligent attention paid to cutting a piece of fruit before. "My dad was a county sheriff, killed in the line of duty. My mother died a couple years later of a broken heart, I think. It was like she simply lost her will to enjoy life after Dad passed."

"Something similar happened with my mom. But it was her mind that went. She lived in a care facility for a while because I wasn't able to nurse her like she needed when I was in college."

Jay glanced up. "I'm sorry." His gaze held hers and for the first time that night, she felt a connection. She eased out a breath. This was fine. Everything was going to be fine.

He had kind eyes. Warm hazel with maple flecks. His lips tilted.

"This is nice. A guy could get used to making dinner with a beautiful lady." There was a keen interest in the way his gaze swept over her that put her feminine sensibilities on alert.

She gave him a squint. "Just wait until I put you to work washing dishes. Then you'll reconsider."

He chuckled and offered a wink. "Not if you're standing by my side."

She cleared her throat and reached for the tomatoes. "How did you decide to become an officer?" Maybe the change to a more serious topic would send him the right message. She didn't want him to think there could be anything more between them.

The paradox of that thought hit her. Why was she longing for the non-existent attention of one handsome officer, but not willing to even consider it with another? She pushed the question aside, realizing that she'd missed the first half of Jay's answer.

"...so all that to say, I guess I was following in my dad's footsteps."

"I'm sure he would be proud of you." She let the conversation trail away then, content to let the silence ride.

He was polite for the rest of the evening, and she felt certain he'd accepted her unspoken message, but part way through the meal he grew silent and a little sullen. For reasons Camryn couldn't put her finger on, her tension slowly climbed back to the height of its previous peak.

As soon as they were done eating and she'd cleaned up the dishes, she excused herself to go to her room.

And when she got there, she locked the door.

Chapter 14

Camryn had finally been able to relax the evening before once she heard Holden return just after ten. She'd had a better night, but still woke early and couldn't fall back to sleep. Finally giving up on the hope of more rest, she rose and showered, then padded down to the kitchen.

Hopefully some more of her packages would arrive today. Last night before falling to sleep, she'd hand-washed some of her new clothes and laid them out to dry. It felt wonderful to be dressed in something besides Holden's baggy things, even if it was only a pair of jeans and a sweater.

She set his credit card in the middle of the kitchen island, wanting to remind herself to give it back to him. She'd felt it in the pocket of his sweats this morning when she'd changed out of them.

Holden wasn't up. She looked around the kitchen, debating the merits of making herself at home, but then decided she could call it a return for his kindness if she fixed breakfast. A cast-iron skillet sitting on the back burner of the stove triggered her memory of her grandmother's German pancakes and blueberry compote.

The fridge didn't reveal any blueberries, but there was a tub of strawberries that would be just as good. And it did contain the eggs and milk she needed.

She was halfway through the meal preparation when Holden stepped into the room. He yawned massively and scrubbed his hands over his face and through his hair, causing several tufts to poke out at odd angles. His bare feet protruded below the cuffs of hip-slung jeans and a taut black T-shirt drew her attention to the play of shadow and light over an appealingly-sculpted torso.

She swiped a wrist across her damp forehead. Was it getting hot in here? This new sweater must be warmer than others she was used to. She resisted a self-deprecating roll of her eyes.

It was only when he propped his hands on his hips and settled an inscrutable gaze on her that she considered she might have misjudged her welcome in a near-stranger's kitchen.

She wrinkled her nose. "Sorry if I overstepped."

"Not at all." He shook his head.

"Oh. The way you were looking at me, I kind of thought I might have?"

He roughed a hand through his hair and looked toward the coffee pot. "Ah no. I was just thinking... Never mind. I'll make coffee."

Okay then. What had that been about?

After he'd filled the basket with grounds, he glanced over at her. "You look nice." He banged the lid of the coffee pot down as though irritated.

"Thank you." Camryn returned her focus to her task, willing away the warmth in her cheeks, and reminding herself not to make more of his obviously grudging compliment than it was. If not grudging, it had certainly been taciturn. She only wished she knew why.

The oven appeared to have reached the right temperature. She popped the skillet in and set the timer, then set to wiping up the counter and putting ingredients away. Several times she and Holden had to swap positions, but they worked seamlessly and silently together.

After he got the coffee going, he hovered near the pot like a vulture.

She grinned at him as she sliced strawberries. "Does it drip faster when you glare at it?"

His lips quirked. "I'm one hundred and five percent certain that it does."

She chuckled and was turning her attention back to her task when she felt the knife bite into her thumb. She gasped and dropped the blade. It clattered into the sink.

"You all right?" He was by her side in an instant, leaning past her shoulder.

She turned on the faucet and thrust her thumb beneath the water. "Yes. I'll be fine. It's not that bad."

"Uh-huh. The water's turning red." He snatched a handful of paper towels. "Here." He took her hand and pressed the towels firmly around her thumb. Then his focus honed in on her face. "How's your pain?"

She squirmed beneath his concern and looked away. "I'm sure it's only cut a little. I really don't feel much. I'm more bothered that I might have ruined the strawberries."

"Don't worry about that. There's plenty in the bowl. The few on the cutting board won't be a big loss."

He bent over her hand and eased the paper towels away from her thumb.

Blood immediately oozed and he clamped the compress tight again, lifting his gaze to hers once more. Concern furrowed his brow. "I think this needs stitches."

She shook her head. The last thing she needed was to spend money on frivolous medical bills. "I really don't think it cut that deep. I must have clipped it in the wrong spot. Let's just wrap it with some padding and a tight Band-Aid and see if the bleeding will stop on its own."

His lips thinned. "If I didn't need to keep you hidden, I'd insist that we go to the clinic right away. But as it stands, I think you might be right."

"Of course I'm right. Don't you know the lady is always right?" She smiled, hoping to ease his tension.

But when he smiled back at her and said softly, "I'll have to remember that," it only caused her pulse to skitter erratically.

He was still standing close, her hand held firmly in his own. His gaze roved from her hairline, to her cheeks, then flicked up to meet her glance.

Her mouth felt dry. She darted her tongue across her lips and held her breath, summoning all her willpower to remember she'd only met the man a few days ago and that, especially from his perspective, this was a business relationship and nothing more. Yet, if he truly felt that way, why was he looking at her like this?

What could it hurt to see if they had something here? Maybe they could make a relationship work? She'd certainly be willing to try.

As if he'd read her thoughts, his gaze lowered to her lips, and for a moment the world all around them seemed frozen. But then he blinked, cleared his throat, and stepped back. "Here. You hold this." He wrapped her free hand around the paper towels. "I'll go get the Band-Aids and ointment and be right back." He left, practically on the run.

Camryn blew out a breath and sagged against the counter. She'd obviously been deprived of close relationships for too long if she'd thought even for a moment the man might step out from behind the shield of his duty.

By the time he returned, she had gathered herself. Resigned herself to the fact that he obviously had no interest in pursuing anything. It was fine. She was used to being alone. It wouldn't kill her.

He worked quickly to help her bandage her thumb, and the timer for the pancake went off just as he finished.

She smiled at him. "Thanks. If you don't mind grabbing that from the oven, I'll get the bowl of good strawberries and meet you at the table."

He nodded. "Can do."

Holden set the cast-iron skillet in the middle of the table, eyeing the steamy golden dough that had partially climbed the sides of the pan. It looked delicious. Was certainly nice to have a woman in the kitchen. As good as bacon and eggs were, that was about the limit of his culinary skills for breakfast.

He glanced up as she set two mugs and the coffee pot on the table, her thumb jutted off to one side. He really needed to have that talk with her that he'd been putting off.

She went back to the kitchen for the bowl of strawberries and a small pitcher of cream.

By the time she returned and sank into her seat, he was ready. "Listen, Camryn…"

She met his gaze, brows slightly arched.

"In the kitchen… I need you to know it's not that I don't find you attract—"

"You don't need to explain. It's okay." She looked out the window, cheeks pink.

"No, I really do. You see, I do find you attractive. But that can only complicate things since I'm supposed to protect you. Letting emotions get involved could make me overlook something I shouldn't." He swallowed. "I know that from experience. Understand?"

Slowly she pulled her attention back to him. "You lost someone?"

He nodded. Turned his coffee cup in circles. Concentrated hard on compartmentalizing the emotions this topic always dredged up.

"I'm sorry. That must have been hard."

"More so because it was my fault."

She tilted her head. "I can't imagine that's true."

He studied the dusting of powdered sugar she'd put on the strawberries. "She was naïve of the danger her father's political leanings had put her in. She liked to shop. I told her not to go, but I fell asleep and she left to go to her favorite boutique." He clamped his teeth hard.

"She should have listened to you."

He nodded. "But I shouldn't have fallen asleep. I relaxed. Thought she would comply because of what we meant to each other."

Camryn lifted a knife and cut a generous portion of the thick pancake from the pan and set it on his plate. "I promise not to do anything you tell me not to do. How's that? I mean—" Her eyes widened. "Not that I have aspirations of us meaning anything to each other or...you know...anything." She couldn't seem to look him in the face.

He fiddled with the fork by his plate. She was entirely too adorable.

She continued to babble. "I simply want you to know you don't have to worry about me not doing what you say. And I really do understand everything you're saying."

He felt himself relax a little. She'd taken all this a lot better than he'd expected her to. "Good. Thank you."

She smiled and handed him the bowl of strawberries. "How did your portion of the watch go last night?"

A segue so he could move on from the painful past. He appreciated that.

"It was dull. Exactly the way I like it." He scooped some berries onto his plate and then handed the bowl to her. "Did Jay behave himself?"

She seemed deeply intent on spreading berries evenly over her pancake. And she was blushing again.

His stomach curled. "Uh-huh. Just as I thought. The kid is a professional flirt."

She twirled a forkful of pancake in some strawberry juice and lifted her gaze to him. "You don't have to worry about me falling for his wiles. I'm not interested in him."

And for some reason, even though he'd just told her they couldn't have a relationship, her statement filled him with relief.

The rest of breakfast was a bit strained, and he was happy to finish the last of his meal and see her do the same.

He stood and took her plate. "Just sit. That thumb of yours doesn't need to get wet. I'll do the dishes."

She rose with him and picked up the strawberry bowl and the pitcher of cream. "I can help with some of it. There's plenty to do that won't require me to get my hands wet. It was me who made the mess in there, after all."

"But it was me who got to enjoy your cooking." He smiled, hoping to return to a measure of their camaraderie from the past couple days. But she was already headed to the kitchen. Again, he half expected her to set her things down and leave, but she stayed, making a couple return trips to clear the table while he loaded the dishwasher.

They moved together as though they had done this a thousand times before. And the chore was finished before he was ready to part from her company. But they both had work to do, and he had to admit that the less time he spent with her, the better it would be for both of them.

Besides, he still needed to finish looking over the files in Lexington and Packard's dirty cop cases. From what he'd seen, they were right. Someone in their department had to be on the take, but so far, he hadn't found a clue as to who it might be.

Tonight's meeting took place in the empty basement of a closed-down theater.

Soren Bane arrived first. Carter Cranston puffed in a few minutes later.

But there was a third presence at this meeting. An iPad sat on a rickety table and the face of Kirk Vossler filled the screen.

Soren and Carter stood side by side, facing the table.

"You're late." Vossler glowered.

Cranston brushed the comment away, without concern. "Had an unavoidable meeting go long. Nothing I could do about it."

"Don't forget who's padding your pockets with this deal." Vossler's beady eyes glittered from the screen.

Soren snorted. "None of this would be possible if you didn't have us, Vossler, and don't you forget it. We're the ones who've done all the legwork."

Cranston glanced at him.

He shrugged. Just because they weren't normally on the same side of anything didn't mean he was going to let this crook Vossler think he was the one running this show. They were all running it, whether he hated his partners or not.

"Is everything set?" Vossler's tone was that of a man trying to regain the upper hand.

Soren met Carter's gaze. "My people are set."

Carter nodded. "Mine too."

"Excellent." Vossler rubbed his hands. "Then I wish each of you well and offer my congratulations on the wealth each of you will soon be inundated with."

Soren withheld a snort. It would be years yet before any of them saw a huge profit from this. But he was willing to wait. Building wealth took time. "Keep your ears tuned to the news. By this time tomorrow, the first step will be complete."

He reached out and shut off the Zoom call without giving Vossler time to respond. Another little message to him that he wasn't the one in charge.

Cranston chuckled. He held out a hand. "All the best to you, Soren. Too bad we part ways here, because, surprised as I am to say it, I'm coming to appreciate you."

Soren nodded. And for the first time, he actually felt a measure of camaraderie with the man next to him. He took the man's hand. "Best of success."

With that, he tucked the iPad beneath his arm and they parted ways, each exiting the building from different doors.

Kirk Vossler rubbed his hands in anticipation.

He decided to order a full course meal from the steak house down the street. Thankfully, his time in jail hadn't been totally wasted. Setting up a few fake accounts was currently giving him some options he wouldn't otherwise have. He pulled up Uber Eats on his phone and typed in his order.

Then he sank against his pillows to wait.

This was it. Years of planning would either succeed or fail in the next twenty-four hours.

When the driver knocked on his door, he called for him just to leave the bag. After he heard the man's footsteps retreating, he tugged on a ski-cap, flipped the light off, then opened the door a spare inch to make sure the driver truly had walked away.

Seeing that the coast was clear, he opened the door only enough to pull the bag into the room before he slammed it shut and quickly thrust the bolt home.

He chuckled at himself. This life on the lam wasn't so bad. He'd escaped much more easily than he'd thought he would. He'd get used to the tension soon enough.

But it was killing him to be only a couple miles from home. There were things there he needed. People he wanted to see.

And this hotel room was starting to feel an awful lot like a different sort of jail cell.

Maybe tomorrow he'd do a test to see if anyone around here would still recognize him.

Maybe a walk down to the corner store to buy toothpaste.

He could pull that off, couldn't he?

His stomach did a flip at the mere thought.

Better safe than sorry. He'd stay in his room and give everything a few more days to calm down.

Chapter 15

When Camryn came down the next morning, Holden was in the living room watching the news.

He glanced over and put the TV on mute. "Morning. You went to bed early last night." His gaze skimmed over the new bohemian top she'd paired with warm leggings and a pink knit scarf. His jaw bulged and he looked away.

She folded her arms, feeling self-conscious. Once again, she'd spent the evening with Jay while Holden drove out to the stakeout. She hadn't gotten any uncomfortable vibes from Jay the night before, but her string of sleepless nights had caught up to her, sending her to her room before Holden had returned from his watch.

"The homemade pizza you left in the fridge was delicious. Thanks."

She pressed her lips together and gave him a nod.

On the screen, a brunette reporter wearing a red dress stood on a downtown city street, speaking into a mic. A large crowd streamed behind her.

Holden unmuted the TV.

"...peaceful gathering of the EPRE, which stands for Everett People for Racial Equality. As you can see behind me, there are people from every race and nationality in this crowd. And so far, John, the protest truly has been the peaceful demonstration it claimed it would be."

"Thank you, Susan. Stay safe out there."

The business-suited reporter at a studio desk was unfamiliar to Camryn. She usually tuned in to large national stations if she ever took time to watch the news. "Is this a local station?" she asked as she sank onto the lip of the recliner.

He nodded. "There's a protest happening in Everett right now. I wanted to tune in to see how it was going. These things always put me on edge. All it takes is one bozo to turn the whole thing on its head. Thankfully, so far they appear to be maintaining civility."

He reached for the remote and was pointing it at the TV when, on the small screen behind the reporter at the desk, a flash of something arched through the air, and then flames exploded on the side of a building.

"No." Holden slumped against the couch, the remote forgotten.

The studio reporter swore on live television. "Cut back to Susan. Cut back to Susan!"

Immediately on the heels of the first incendiary, several more were thrown against other buildings. The crowd burgeoned into bedlam in the blink of an eye. On the street, the reporter and her cameraman were apparently running for their lives from the way the video jagged and came in and out of focus.

The red sleeve of the brunette's dress was visible to the left of the screen. "John, things have...just...dissolved...into chaos here," she puffed.

Billows of smoke filled the screen. People screamed. A siren squawked. The reporter stumbled and fell to the sidewalk.

"I've got you," a voice said.

The camera jounced and spun and then went still, with its focus pointed down the length of the sidewalk as the cameraman apparently helped the reporter to her feet.

Camryn leaned forward. "Oh, my goodness!" She pointed toward the flaming restaurant in the back of the shot. "That's D & J's Diner! The restaurant where I work!" She moaned. "Or maybe I should say worked. Oh, poor Jean and David. They've owned that diner since the late eighties."

Despite her sorrow for her employers, she couldn't help a fleeting selfish thought. Now what was she going to do about her looming bills?

Holden leaned forward, tension filling every angle of his body. His attention was still severely focused on the news when his phone rang. He glanced at the screen, then answered. "Hey Jay, you watching the news?"

Camryn lost sight of the diner as the cameraman picked up the camera and resumed chasing the reporter away from the carnage. Now her jog had a distinct limp to it. She was running barefoot and her high-heeled shoes were clutched in one hand.

"Sure." Holden frowned. "That would be fine." His gaze slipped away from the news and landed on Camryn.

Her tension rose. The puzzlement in Holden's gaze made her stomach clench. "What?" she mouthed.

He snapped his focus to the floor at his feet. "Sure, Jay. Anytime, you know that." He was silent for a moment, then, "Yeah. I know. This situation in Everett is going to get uglier before it gets better."

Camryn swallowed. She wasn't sure what was going on, but there was a note in Holden's tone that she didn't like. She pressed a hand over the ache in her stomach.

Holden hung up and tossed his phone onto the couch. He rose and immediately set to pacing, thrusting his fingers back through his hair.

"What?"

"I'm not sure. Jay says he needs to talk to me right away. He's coming here now."

"Talk about what?"

He gripped the back of his neck, still pacing. "He didn't say. Only that it was about Kate. I hope she hasn't talked." A muscle bulged in his jaw.

Camryn's neck ached. "I'm sure it will be fine." She wasn't certain at all.

He propped his hands on his hips and looked at her, coming to a standstill. "Maybe. But there's something I want to show you, in case you need it." He motioned that she should follow him. He led her through to the back of the house, then paused by the back door, assessing the sky outside. "It's cold today."

"I'll just run up and grab my jacket."

"Okay. I'll wait." He lifted a leather jacket from a coat tree by the back door for himself.

It only took her a minute to get her coat. She slipped it on, then followed him across the stone patio. Her breath fogged the air before her and her curiosity couldn't be vanquished. What could he want to show her out here?

She tucked her chin into the collar of her coat, subtly taking in the pleasing sight of his broad shoulders and trim hips as he strode before her. Her lips tilted. To maintain this view, she'd follow him through the frozen tundra if need be.

If only they weren't walking toward the water. She pressed her lips together. Her fear was totally irrational, she knew. It wasn't like the water was going to leap out of its boundary and drag her under.

He led the way down the hill in the direction of the clearing where they'd landed that first day. When he reached it, he stopped and drew her to him, pointing her in the direction he was facing. "Here."

Behind them, the ocean lapped at the shore, and she couldn't stop a quick check to make sure they were still a good distance from the water.

He hesitated. "You're trembling."

She gave a self-deprecating chuckle. "I'm not so good around water, if you'll recall."

His thumbs worked gently into her shoulder muscles. "Bad experience at some point?"

She swallowed, reminding herself that the warm hands on her shoulders were only there out of duty. "Yes. When I was ten, the older brother of a friend held me under the water at the neighborhood pool because his sister had told him I bullied her and stole her lunch money."

Holden leaned to look down at her face. "You stole a girl's lunch money?" One brow lifted. "I can't see you doing that."

"I didn't. But the girl took a disliking to me. Maybe out of jealousy because I'd recently been appointed the captain of our swim team. She lied to her brother about me."

"I see." He retreated behind her once more and now his fingers worked into the tense muscles along her neck. "Did you keep swimming?"

She shook her head. "By the time the lifeguard got to me, they had to perform lifesaving procedures, and I spent a couple days in the hospital. As an adult, I've tried a few times to conquer my fear. I know it's silly."

"It's not silly." Holden kept massaging. "I can't imagine how scared and helpless you felt, being held under the water so long. That's terrible."

For some reason, his acknowledgement of her injustice helped her relax. "Thank you. But I'm sure you didn't bring me down here to talk about my water phobia."

"Right, let's make this quick so you can get back to higher ground." He pointed to a boulder in the hillside below the house, leaning over her shoulder. "See that rock right there with the white scrape on it?"

She nodded.

"There's a hidden cellar down here. If anything happens to me, or if something happens at the house, you come down here to this clearing. The rock will be your marker." He was already leading the way toward the rock. When he reached it, he took one step to the right and then bent to push a large salal bush to one side. Behind it was a door.

Holden glanced at her with a smirk. "This was my dad's get-away-from-it-all place. Sometimes he'd spend the whole day down here. Careful here." He held out a hand to her. "There's quite a step down to the floor."

His hand settled around hers, warm and firm, but he released her as soon as she'd found her footing. She tucked her lower lip between her teeth and folded her arms, noting that he was rubbing his palms against his jeans.

"Uh, so...like I said, if for any reason you don't feel safe at the house, I want you to run here, okay? And you should know that the water never rises this high, not even in a storm."

She appreciated him considering her feelings about that.

He gestured to a shelf along one wall of the dugout. "There's a small kerosene heater to warm it up in here, but don't run it unless you can place it here near the door, which you should leave open a crack. The fumes will build up otherwise. This"—he laid his hand on a sealed plastic tub—"has food in it. Don't worry, I go through it fairly often to make sure it's up to date. And this"—he pointed to another tub—"has first aid supplies. There are two five-gallon jugs of water in the corner there. And you can lock the doors from the inside. You simply slide this bolt. See?" He demonstrated.

Camryn looked at him. She couldn't imagine ever feeling the need to run to this place for safety, but he was probably remembering the past. Maybe because he'd just offered her such reassurance, she wanted to return the favor. She laid a hand on his arm. "I'm sure everything is going to be fine. Even if Kate talked."

He looked down at her. His Adam's apple bobbed. "We still don't know anything. I think that's what worries me most." He covered her hand where it rested on his arm, and his thumb trailed across her knuckles. "Anyone ever taught you cold survival?"

Her eyes widened. "How long do you anticipate I would be down here?"

He shrugged. Shook his head. "We need to be prepared for all scenarios."

As though he'd just realized how close they were standing, he dropped his hand from hers and stepped back. He stretched an arm toward the door. "We need to get back to the house to meet Jay."

He closed the door, then fluffed the branches of the bush, and they stepped back. If she didn't know the door was there, she wouldn't look twice at that area if she were passing.

As Holden led the way back toward the house, he peppered her with instructions.

If she were ever locked out in the cold, she should don as many layers as she could, but not raise a sweat.

Whatever she did, she should not get wet. Her chances of survival dropped to near zero in that case.

He didn't have to worry on that count, she mused.

Drink plenty of water. But don't eat snow. Apparently, it took a lot of energy for a body to work at melting ingested snow. "Around here, that's probably not going to be an issue because we don't get that much snow. But it can get really cold, especially this time of year." He stopped at the back door and faced her. "So, you got all that?"

She couldn't withhold a smile. "If I tell you I promise to watch some YouTube videos about cold-survival, will you be satisfied?"

"No! Do you know how many quacks are out there on YouTube spouting 'truth'?" The air quotes he put around the word *truth* grew her smile.

She ticked off a list on her fingers. "Layers. Don't sweat. Don't get wet. Drink plenty. Don't eat snow even though there isn't likely to be any."

He squeezed her arm. "You're a quick study. We should get inside." Despite his words, he didn't move. He remained looking down at her, one hand still on her arm.

Camryn refused to analyze the way he studied her. She tore her gaze to the zipper pull in the middle of his chest. "If Kate did talk, please don't fire her on account of me."

He released her, stepped back, and held the door open. "I'm hoping that's not the case, but she's spread information she shouldn't have before. She's never been malicious, however, and I specifically told her it could endanger you. So I hope she held her tongue. But if I'm honest, I've been waiting for her to swing her last strike. I just don't know who..." His gaze snapped to hers as she stepped past him into the house. "With your diner burning down, you wouldn't be interested in moving to the island and working for my office, would you? Until we're sure you are out of danger, you can keep working from my place." He stripped off his leather jacket and hooked it on the coat-tree.

Camryn felt her eyes shoot wide. She envisioned the sight of the diner burning in the background on TV. Almost inevitably, she wouldn't have a job to go back to. And even if they rebuilt, it would be months. "You'd really want to hire me? Or is this a pity job?" Despite the warmth of the house, her hands still felt chilled from the biting wind. She thrust them into the pockets of her coat.

With one hand at her back, he nudged her toward the front of the house. "This is not a pity offer. You've been doing a fantastic job with the files. You've made more progress in one day than Kate had in weeks."

"Well... This is all a little fast. What's the rental situation like out here?" And what would the job pay? But thankfully she caught herself before blurting that out.

"How about this. You work for me temporarily until we see what's going to happen with your job in Everett. I know an older woman who has a room she wants to rent."

When he named the price, her jaw dropped. It was one third of what she was paying for her studio apartment in the city now. "Seriously?"

"Seriously. And Mrs. Hutchinson will be absolutely thrilled to have you."

"I'll think about it. I'm going to head up to my room so that when Jay gets here, you'll have some privacy to speak with him. I'll let you know my answer later this evening." She took the stairs, but when she reached the top, she was so preoccupied with trying to decide what the best thing to do might be that she paused, staring at the door to her room in thought.

She thought of all the prayers she'd mentally accused God of not answering. Had He been orchestrating things for her all along? Frustration with her continual lack of faith washed over her. When would she learn to keep her trust in Him even when things didn't seem to be going her way? Once more she offered up the prayer she'd been praying off and on ever since Holden had spoken to her about it. *Lord, help my unbelief.*

She stepped toward her door and was just pulling her hands from her pockets when she felt something hard in one pocket of her jacket. She tugged the object out and frowned at it.

It was a small flash drive.

A flash drive that she'd never seen before.

What was it doing in the pocket of her coat?

Damien got the text from Sheila at the hospital as he was arriving for work the next morning.

With all the craziness surrounding this investigation, he hadn't gotten to see her in the past few days. He texted her back. *I miss you.*

The screen immediately indicated she was typing. Her response came through a moment later. *I know you've been swamped. But I miss you too. Swing by for coffee and **homemade chocolate chip cookies** whenever you can find a few minutes.*

He grinned. *A woman who's willing to give up her favorite brownies in favor of chocolate chip cookies is one worth keeping around.*

She sent back a laughing face, followed by another heart.

See you in a few.

A thumbs-up popped onto the screen.

He forced himself to put the phone in his pocket. She was at work and likely didn't have time to be joking with him about snacks via text.

He stopped by Case's desk. "Wright is awake. We can have five minutes with him this morning."

Case was already grabbing his coat from the back of his chair. "Sheila came through? I confess I didn't think she would. With the new COVID precautions, I didn't think they'd let us talk to him till he was released."

Damien pumped his brows. "Helps to have an insider who happens to like me."

"Miracles still happen," Case offered dryly as he followed Damien to their car.

Sheila met them at the ER entrance and led them through the ICU. She paused beside a curtained bed. "This is it. Just be quick about it and call me when you need to leave. I'll escort you out." She sent a soft look in Damien's direction.

"Thanks." He squeezed her arm and reminded himself to ask her to dinner. He knew she'd broken several hospital rules to allow them in here.

Gandry's eyes widened when he saw them step through the curtain that separated his bed from the others in the ICU. He scrabbled for the nurse's call button.

Damien lifted his hands. "Relax man. We aren't here to finish you off." He kept his voice quiet enough that the hum, whir, and beeps of the hospital machinery throughout the room would keep their conversation private.

Case sank casually onto the end of the man's bed. "We are here to give you a chance to tell us what you know about the hit on Treyvon Johnson the other night."

"How do I know you aren't here to kill me?"

Damien folded his arms. "We're cops. We aren't here to kill you."

Gandry tossed down the call button and pressed his lips together. "Man, you don't know anything."

Case walked him methodically through what they did know. Him borrowing the GTO. It being used in the hit and run. Him getting into it a block away and ending up in the same alley where Ryan Skelly, an officer who'd handled Treyvon's phone, had also been killed. "All this could end up pinned on your shoulders, Wright. Unless you decide to tell us the full story."

"They already tried to kill me. I'm not talking." He rubbed at the surgical bandaging on his chest and seemed to be battling for oxygen.

Damien stepped closer. "That's right. They did try to kill you. But if you talk to us, we'll keep you safe. Put you in protective custody. Make sure they can't get to you."

"Protective custody is exactly where they can, and would, get to me." Wright's eyes widened, as though he realized he'd said too much.

Case maintained his casual position on the end of the bed. "Listen, Wright. We know there are dirty cops involved. But we can't do anything about them without proof. You got the proof we need?"

Gandry maintained his silence, but he at least appeared to be thinking. His mouth worked like he might be thirsty. "I still don't know whether to trust you."

"Would we be conversing with you if we wanted you dead?" Damien picked up the pink water pitcher and poured the man a drink. He handed him the cup. "They tried to kill you. You owe them no loyalty."

Gandry took a couple sips of the water, then set the cup back on his tray. "I'd need immunity."

Damien looked at Case. This could get tricky. In order to get him immunity, they'd need to file paperwork. Paperwork that would let the very cops they were trying to get evidence on know that Wright was talking. "You're going to have to trust us on that, Wright. At least if you want to live."

"Fine. But you have to move me. Right now. Somewhere that only you know the location of."

"We can't do that. You took two bullets through your lungs and had lifesaving surgery. If we move you, you could die."

Gandry shook his head. "You leave me here, and it's only a matter of time before they come for me again. How hard you think it's going to be for them to get to me when I'm moved out of the ICU? The only thing still keeping me alive is that there are too many witnesses in here."

Case lifted a shoulder to Damien as if to say he might agree with that.

Damien pondered as he glanced through the curtain to the nurse's station beyond. Two medical personnel with their backs to him, wearing full protective gear and masks, were speaking to Sheila. She handed back an ID badge with a nod, then jutted her chin their direction.

Case followed his gaze. "Will she do it?"

Damien lifted a hand. "I think so. If I ask. But it looks like orderlies are coming to take him for tests or something. So, it's now or never."

Case stood. "I'll delay the orderlies while you talk to her. Just help me get him out of the bed first." He scooted Gandry's hospital table away and grabbed the wheelchair sitting to one side. "Come on, Gandry. Let's get you out of here."

"Not so fast." The words were spoken softly by one of the orderlies as they stepped through the gap.

Damien froze.

Ed and Gray stood inside the curtain, guns drawn.

Ed's eyes crinkled above the edge of his blue mask. "Howdy, fellas."

Gray focused on Case and Damien. He swung his gun to indicate the curtains that cordoned them off from the rest of the room. "Better cooperate, boys." His threat was clear.

If bullets started flying, any number of people in this unit could be hurt.

Chapter 16

While Holden waited for Jay to arrive, Camryn went down to the office and retrieved the laptop. Back upstairs, she settled on her bed and plugged the flash drive into the port.

There was only one file on the drive.

A video.

She frowned. Where had this drive come from? She double-clicked the file.

It was footage from what looked like a dimly-lit warehouse. A small group of people, huddled close together, spoke furtively to one another, checking over their shoulders often. Whoever recorded this hid from a perch much higher than the group of people, making the audio too quiet to hear.

She pumped the laptop's volume to its max and restarted the video at full screen, leaning closer to try to make out faces of the little group.

Did she know any of these people? She still couldn't figure out how this had come to be in her pocket.

There was a soft scratching sound, like a piece of cloth dragging across a mic, and then the audio rose to an understandable volume.

"…paid and ready to rumble." The speaker was a tall, handsome man with graying hair who was wearing a gray suit. He arched his neck to adjust the red tie at his throat, and for a split second, he faced the camera.

Camryn reached for the trackpad. She stepped the footage back and paused on the man's face. Her lips pursed. Where had she seen him before? He looked so familiar. She snapped a screenshot and uploaded the face to Google's reverse image search engine.

Immediately the site spit out several news articles. The top headline read, *Washington State Republican Senator, Carter Cranston, Reelected!*

Her curiosity spiked. She'd never met the man. What was a video of him doing in her pocket?

She clicked play again. A second man was speaking now. "My people too. Businesses in those blocks will realize it will be foolish to rebuild."

Camryn took a breath. She didn't have to look that man up. She would recognize his voice anywhere. He was a regular at D and J's. Democratic Senator, Soren Bane.

What were those two men doing in a shady meeting together?

The video was only a few minutes long. None of the other four attendees looked up, so she never did get a good look at them. Three were also men. Two in suits and one in a dark uniform of some sort. Police? Security? She couldn't quite tell on the small screen of the laptop, especially in the poorly lit warehouse.

The sixth person at the meeting remained featureless in the shadows, speaking so low that Camryn couldn't make out the words. But all eyes turned toward whoever it was as if looking for instructions.

Camryn wished the audio was better because she kept missing parts of what was said. But she caught mention of October twenty-fifth and realized, with a jolt, that was today!

Her eyes widened. *Ready to rumble...businesses in those blocks...foolish to rebuild.*

Could this be about the riots going on in the city right now? They'd *planned* this?

Another memory flashed. Her kneeling by the injured undercover officer in the street and tugging his hand from her jacket, his fingers tangling with the flap of her pocket.

He had put this in her coat!

A shiver slipped down her spine.

Could this be the reason he'd been killed in the first place? She had to show this to Holden right now!

Damien thrust his hands into the air, seeing Wright do the same. "Easy guys."

Wright cursed softly.

Case straightened from where he'd been unfolding the wheelchair, hands up.

"That's right. Keep your hands where we can see them," Ed spoke softly.

Ed and Gray? Damien felt the betrayal like a gunshot. Miller yes. But he hadn't seen anything suspicious from these two.

He clenched his jaw. This could get tricky. "This is a no-win situation for you, boys. You just going to shoot all three of us and then walk away?"

Ed and Gray exchanged a look.

"What do we do now?" Gray asked. "We were supposed to wheel him out of here under cover."

"We don't panic, that's what," Ed whispered. "We keep to our orders."

"And what are your orders exactly?" Damien asked, edging his voice a little louder.

"Keep your voice down!" Ed's eyes glittered.

Gray gingerly parted the curtain, presumably to see if anyone had heard Damien's words and might be checking on them.

Sheila glanced up from where she was huddled at the ICU desk, talking with several other nurses. Damien met her eyes briefly above Gray's head. She froze. Then the curtain fell back into place.

"I don't like the way that nurse is eyeing us, Ed. We need to get out of here."

Damien swallowed. How much had she seen? He hoped she wouldn't try to come in to see what was going on. He also hoped she'd be concerned enough to at least call hospital security. They needed backup.

Meanwhile they needed to try to get some information. At the very least, keeping the partners talking might throw them off their guard a little and give him and Case a chance to try to regain control.

Ed paced and swore. "This is bad, Gray. How are we going to get out of this one? We can't march all three of them out past the nurse's station."

Case eased a couple steps toward one side of the partition.

Damien took his cue and slid toward the other. Making them split their focus would give the best advantage. If not for putting others at risk, they could fight back. But as it stood, any resistance they might offer would end up getting innocent people hurt.

"Both of you freeze," Ed snapped quietly. Sweat glistened on his forehead, despite the comfortable temperature of the room. "Packard, don't move. Lexington, hand me your gun, nice and easy."

Case met Damien's gaze as he eased his Glock from its holster.

"What made you boys come by, anyhow?" Damien threw out the dry question, hoping to distract them and maybe give Case a chance to act while he still had his gun, but neither of the officers fell for the ploy.

Gray kept his gun trained between Damien and Wright, while Ed secured Case's gun. And then both men turned their focus on him.

Damien cringed and carefully tugged his gun from his holster.

Once his weapon was secured, Gray smiled. "The reason we stopped by is easy," he said, gaze swinging to Wright. "Our orders were to make sure Wright here didn't rat us out."

"Which, it seems, is exactly what he was doing." Gray glowered. "So it's a good thing we arrived when we did. We paid you well, Wright. You weren't going to rat on us, were you?"

Gandry flopped his head back against the pillow. "Doesn't matter if I was or wasn't, now does it? You boys are gonna do what you're gonna do."

Damien took a step forward. "Well, it seems we are at an impasse. You can't just shoot us and walk away. You'd be gunned down before you even left the premises. Besides, you know there are security cameras all over in here."

Ed offered a thin smirk. "Don't get too cocky. You have no idea how high our friendships go."

"Miller?" Damien took a stab in the dark. "If he's as high as your friendships go, I hate to break it to you, but that's not very high." He held his breath. Would the ploy work?

Gray chuckled. "Miller is low man on the totem pole."

"Gray, shut it!" Ed's whisper was furious.

Gray's face turned serious as he must have suddenly realized what he'd given away.

Damien met Case's gaze. So Miller *was* part of all this. And by their "high friendships" did they mean the captain? His gut ached at the thought. How many investigations had he and Case worked with the man?

The curtain to the cubicle was suddenly swept aside. "Okay Mr. Wright, time for your— Oh!" Sheila focused on the guns, eyes shooting wide.

Damien's heart fell at the same time curiosity tugged at his brow. He'd hoped to keep her out of this, but if she'd thought Ed and Gray were orderlies who'd come to take Wright for some assessments, why would she come in as she had?

With a clipboard in one hand, she lifted her palms. She stepped to Damien's side of the now partially-revealed cubical, putting her back to him while keeping Ed and Gray before her.

At the desk, one of the other nurses looked up and cried out. "Guns! They have guns!"

Ed was quick to act. "That's right we do." He swept the curtain all the way open and stepped into the center of the ICU, weapon raised. "I'm a police officer. Everyone, stay calm."

No one did.

Screams and gasps emanated from all the staff. People dove for whatever cover they could find. Across the room, one of the patient's machines sent a piercing alarm through the unit.

Ed put his gun in the face of a screaming nurse and yelled for her to shut up.

Gray demanded another nurse deal with the alarm.

Damien felt a warm hand on his and looked down to see that Sheila had reached behind her to grab his hand. She kept her back to him and guided his hand to the waistband of her scrubs where he felt a cool, round cylinder.

He tugged it free and a quick glance showed that it was a can of mace.

Bless her. The woman was a genius.

Damien didn't waste any time. He swept Sheila behind him with one arm and strode up behind Gray, who was nearest. "Hey, Gray."

The man turned and Damien gave him a good dose of the spray right in the eyes.

He screamed and clawed at his face, dropping his gun.

Damien swept it up and leveled it on Ed, who was turning to see what Gray was screaming about. "Drop your gun, Ed. Do it now."

"Like he—"

The screaming nurse went suddenly quiet, whipped out her own canister of mace, and sprayed Ed's face.

The bellow Ed loosed was loud enough to rival a boisterous woman in labor.

Case was on him inside a second and stripped him of his weapon. "On the floor, Ed. Hands behind your back."

Damien did the same to Gray, and within moments, they had both men restrained.

Damien turned to Sheila. He wrapped one arm around her shoulders and tugged her close. "That was some quick thinking."

She rested her head on his shoulder for a brief second. "Thanks. We have to be quick thinkers around here."

"How did you know we needed help?"

"Please." She grinned up at him. "A woman always knows when her man needs help."

"Her man, huh?" He arched a brow.

She offered a cheeky grin, then patted his chest in farewell. "Their badges checked out, but I'd never seen them before and neither had any of the other nurses. One orderly might be new, but they'd never send two brand new guys together. Then, when I saw your face, I knew something was wrong."

"You're a genius. How about you let me take you to dinner as thanks?" He held his breath. Would she turn him down?

She smiled. "I'd like that. Text me the time and place. Meanwhile, I better get these two treated." She resumed her all-business attitude as she squatted next to the still moaning and sniffling officers.

Damien assessed Gandry. His heartrate monitor was beeping so fast that it was difficult to tell one beat from the next. His bandaged chest heaved, and his eyes continued to dart around the room like he still wasn't one hundred percent certain he was safe.

Damien stepped to the side of his bed and dropped one hand against his shoulder. "You're safe now, Wright."

Maybe now the man would be less reluctant to tell his story.

Damien met Case's gaze across the room.

They both released a breath.

This had been too close for comfort.

Jay hadn't arrived yet when Camryn went downstairs to see if Holden was free.

She found him pacing in the living room. "Everything okay?"

He glanced up. "Jay said he was leaving the office when he called. He should have been here thirty minutes ago. No answer on his cell. And no answer at the office either."

"I'm fine to stay here alone if you need to go look for him."

He swiped away the offer. "Could be any number of explanations. I'm sure he'll be here soon."

"I need to show you something." She explained how she'd found the USB drive in her coat pocket and that she thought the murdered undercover officer had put it there.

His brows shot up.

She turned the laptop toward him. "It only has this video on it. I think it's about today's riots."

"What?"

"Yeah." Her heart sank. If only she'd found the drive earlier, she could have probably prevented a lot of destruction. "Just watch it."

Holden plugged in a pair of headphones and then watched the video while Camryn paced and studied him for his reaction.

When he finished, his face was grave. "I need to get this to Lexington and Packard right away. Two of these guys are state politicians and another is a uniformed officer. I can't tell who the other two in suits are or the one in the shadows. But maybe the lab at the precinct will be able to do some enhancing." His gaze wandered to the front window, a frown pinching his brow.

"If you won't go look for Jay on your own, then let me come with you." She swiped a gesture to the video. "Doesn't this prove that they won't be coming after me now? I mean, if they were worried Treyvon told me about the riots, they're happening now, so they no longer need to worry, right?"

Holden pondered. "Maybe."

"I don't understand why they would want to instigate riots?"

"Money." His lips thinned. "It's always about money."

"How do they make money off a riot?"

"There could be a number of ways, but the biggest one that comes to mind is it would cause property values to plummet. Combined with people wanting to sell and get out as quickly as they can. People with money could snap all that real estate up and make a hefty profit down the road."

"That's terrible. All those small business owners like David and Julie, out of business."

"Yeah." Holden clicked a few keys on the laptop. He picked up his phone, touched the screen a few times and then tucked it between his ear and shoulder as he continued to work on the laptop.

Faintly, she could hear the phone ringing on the other end. But it must have gone to voice mail because Holden set the phone down without speaking.

Outside, tires clattered over the stone-paved driveway. Camryn glanced through the window. Jay's cruiser pulled to a stop, bright sunlight glinting off the windshield. "Oh, Jay's here."

Holden blew out a breath that revealed how worried he'd been. "Good." He pressed a few more keys on the keyboard and then rose from the desk. "Let's see what his delay was."

He stepped onto the porch, but Camryn didn't follow. She didn't want Jay to get any wrong impressions about how much he meant to her. In fact, she should return upstairs so he and Holden could have their privacy.

She scooted into the entry, intent on taking the stairs before they came back in, but the sight that greeted her froze her in her tracks.

Kate stood on the threshold with a gun pointed at Holden's chest.

Chapter 17

Damien sat next to Case, across the table from Ed. Gray waited in the next room over. Damien was content to sit back and let Case drive the interrogation, but so far, the only words Ed had spoken were, "I want my lawyer."

So now they were waiting for the lawyer to arrive. He had apparently been delayed in court—a tactic Damien guessed was more about figuring out a plan than actually being in court, though that was only a guess.

He nudged Case with the back of his hand. "Let's talk to Gray. Maybe he'll be willing to cut a deal."

Ed's jaw bunched, but he remained silent.

Flanked by officers Miller and Kingston, Captain Danielson stormed toward Damien and Case as they exited, fists balled, neck tendons taut. "There better be a good explanation for why you have two of my detectives in interrogation rooms!"

Damien studied the man, his earlier questions rising once more to the surface. Was the captain crooked? His recent behavior—especially his standing up for dirty cops—certainly gave pause. And yet, if *he* were suspected of something underhanded, wouldn't he want his captain to go to bat for him?

"Yes, sir. There is." Case spoke calmly. "I took the liberty of having the hospital send you some footage, sir."

Damien transferred his gaze to Officer Miller and his partner Jack Kingston, who both stood a few paces away. Miller couldn't seem to meet his gaze, but Kingston's gaze was clear and direct. Interesting. The two had only been partners for a couple weeks, if he recalled correctly. Miller's feet shifted as he studied the ground near Damien. Though Gray had mentioned him, they couldn't arrest the man on hearsay. But he had to know his neck was in a noose. It came as a surprise that he was even showing his face in the precinct. But maybe he'd just arrived for his shift and was only now hearing the news.

"With me!" Captain Danielson barked at them. He started toward his office but then froze. His gaze swept the precinct, before he resumed his trek.

Leaving every other officer standing in frozen silence, Case and Damien followed the captain into his office and closed the door. The man didn't even bother to sit down but propped one hand on his desk and jiggled his mouse from a standing position. After a couple clicks, he stilled, and Damien could see the hospital video footage reflected in the captain's glasses. The video ended, but the captain didn't move. He kept staring at his screen.

Damien waited, somehow feeling like a kid who had stopped a fight and still been the one sent to the principal's office.

After a few seconds of silence, the captain grunted and then swore. "Unbelievable."

Damien waited, wondering if he meant their arrest of the officers was unbelievable, or if Ed and Gray were unbelievable. The way the captain had been coaster-riding lately, it could go either way.

For several minutes, the captain paced and swore and paced some more. Finally, he stopped before the window in his office that overlooked the city and propped both hands on his hips. "Sorry. I'm handling this badly."

Damien looked at Case.

He lifted one shoulder.

Captain Danielson sighed. "My wife passed away last night."

Damien felt the shock of the words hit him like a blast. And at the same time, he was washed with a wave of relief. This would explain why the captain had been acting so strange lately, wouldn't it? He wasn't a crook. He was simply doing his best to keep his life together under terrible circumstances. "I'm so sorry, sir. I knew she was sick, but I had no idea..."

The captain remained in his position, looking out the window. "I didn't want the men to make a big fuss." He pulled in a stuttering breath, held it for a moment, and then blew it out through pursed lips. "No idea how I'm going to survive without her."

Case approached and settled a hand on the man's shoulder. "What can we do to help?"

Damien's appreciation for his partner rose. Case always was better in these situations.

The captain kept looking out the window, but his hand did rise to touch Case's briefly. "Just find all the dirty cops in my department. Root them out."

Case nodded and stepped back. "You should know, sir, that Gray has already implicated Lawrence Miller."

The captain sighed. "Fine. Hold him for questioning. Kingston too."

"I don't think we should do that, sir." Damien surprised even himself with the words.

The captain spun on him. "Why not?"

Damien ran a hand over his face. "I'm not certain I have a good answer, sir, other than..." He shrugged. "With that jail break, and the riots, I feel like this is a lot of random unusual things all happening at once. Makes me wonder if they aren't tied together. Maybe Miller will panic and lead us to something."

The captain brushed a hand through the air absentmindedly. "Fine. Have them followed. But whatever you do, don't lose them."

"Kate? What's the meaning of this?" Holden asked, hands raised to shoulder level. He sidestepped and Camryn didn't miss the fact that the movement put him between her and Kate.

Camryn's heart was beating so hard she could feel it pounding against her ribs. She'd never had a gun pointed in her direction before. She peeked from under his arm.

Holden shifted and Kate took a quick step back. "Don't move. I mean it."

He stilled. "You're going to have to explain."

She motioned with the gun. "Into the living room. Both of you."

Holden reached back and nudged Camryn to precede him, keeping his body between her and Kate's gun. She scuttled into the living room, eyes darting for any weapon she might grab. But nothing was close enough.

"Sit!" Kate snapped. "Wait!"

They froze.

She swung her gun from Camryn to Holden's ankle. "He always keeps a pistol strapped to his ankle. Get it carefully. And if you make any sudden moves, I won't hesitate to shoot you both."

Camryn despaired. *Please Lord, don't let me get Holden shot.*

She slowly lifted the cuff of his jeans, pulled the pistol from his ankle holster, and held it away from her body with two fingers so Kate could see she wasn't going to try anything with it.

Kate motioned. "Toss it to me."

Camryn darted Holden a glance. "Will it fire?"

He shook his head and motioned that she should do as Kate said.

She tossed the gun onto the floor at Kate's feet, feeling as if she was throwing their last chance at life away. Then she sank onto the couch, and Holden sat right next to her, taking her hand. She laced her fingers with his, relishing in the comfort that small gesture gave her in this situation.

Camryn heard Holden swallow.

They both looked at Kate.

She paced the carpet, gun loosely trained on them, muttering to herself.

Holden shifted slightly. "Whatever is going on, Kate, we can help you. But you need to put the gun down so we can talk."

She spun to face him, pistol extended and trembling. "Shut up! I don't want to hear any of your negotiation talk!" Her gaze slipped to their intertwined hands. "Oh! So she's already woven herself around you like poison ivy, has she?"

Camryn's heart jolted at the venomous words. Much as Holden's hand comforted, it was obviously causing Kate to degenerate even more. She eased her hand out of his grasp and onto her lap.

Holden rubbed his palms on his knees. "We're just a little stressed here, Kate. Understandable with you waving a gun at us, wouldn't you say?"

Kate didn't answer. She resumed her distressed pacing and muttering. "I...killed...him. I think...I...killed him. He...looked... dead." She shook her head. "No. He can't be dead. He'll be fine. Maybe...he'll be fine."

Camryn felt her eyes widen as she met Holden's brief glance. She thought of Jay's car, the one Kate pulled into the driveway a few minutes ago. Was he the one who was dead?

"Who will be fine, Kate?" Holden, leaned forward, easing closer to the lip of the couch. He looked like a panther about to pounce.

"My son. My...only...son."

Holden's brow furrowed. "You don't have a son, Kate."

She spun on him, face contorted with rage. "Yes, I do..." Her face crumpled. "Did have a son."

For a brief moment, Camryn thought Kate would lose the strength from her legs. She swayed, gripping her head with both hands, the gun dangerously close to her temple.

"Let me help you, Kate. I can help you." Holden held out a hand, palm up, silently entreating her to give him the gun.

She blinked a couple times and then, as though a veil had been lifted, her gaze hardened and she straightened. Her glittering ire zeroed in on Holden once more. And when she spoke, bits of spittle flew from her mouth. "You don't know anything, Holden Parker. Shut up and let me think."

Holden's jaw tightened. His hands fisted and unfisted restlessly.

Camryn settled a hand against his to draw his attention. She nodded toward Kate and mouthed, *Shall I try?*

He roughed a hand over the lower half of his face, then raised it as if to say, what could it hurt?

Camryn moistened her lips. She looked at Kate. "Who was your son?"

Her face contorted with grief. "Jay. My baby boy."

Camryn felt all the blood drain from her face. Kate *had* killed Jay! From the look on Holden's face, he'd had no idea she was Jay's mother. Jay had said he'd been adopted. Was Kate the woman who'd chosen alcohol over her child?

Kate's countenance twisted into a snarl, and she advanced a step toward Camryn. "And this is all your fault."

Camryn despaired. Maybe Kate was right. If she hadn't revealed herself to the woman, would all this be happening right now? Holden had asked her to remain hidden, but she'd done the same thing the woman he'd lost had done. She'd discounted his advice and gone against it.

She worked some moisture into her mouth before she was able to manage. "Why did you kill him?"

Kate continued to pace, shaking her head. "Why didn't he do as I told him? If he'd done what he was supposed to do, none of this would have been necessary."

"What was he supposed to do?" Holden's voice sounded like twelve-grit sandpaper.

Kate ignored them. Paced. Muttered.

Holden leaned even farther forward on the couch, and Camryn noticed he was gripping the bottom edge of the hefty wooden coffee table.

He glanced over at her. With a jut of his chin he indicated the door beside them that led through to the dining room. He gave a quick check at Kate and then mouthed. *When I move, you run. Remember?* His brows lifted slightly.

She nodded. She should run to the dugout shelter. But she didn't have a coat. She'd taken it off upstairs and left it on her bed. No matter. She wouldn't be there long. Only until Holden could get Kate into custody. Unless...

She dropped a hand onto his arm and gave a little shake of her head. She didn't want him getting hurt. Kate could shoot him. They should figure a way out of this together.

"Remember your promise," he said softly.

She blew out a tremulous breath. Her promise that she would listen to him. She'd broken it once already. She didn't want to do it again.

His eyes narrowed. And he jutted his chin toward the door with more force.

Camryn gave a nod. She would do as he asked.

And then Kate pivoted and he moved.

Kate's back was to them for a fraction of a second. Holden picked up the coffee table and charged toward her, thrusting it before him like a shield and a club all in one.

Camryn lurched for the door.

She'd only gotten two steps into the dining room when Kate screeched.

And then gunfire shattered the air.

A loud crash followed.

Despite her promise, Camryn froze. She glanced back. And gasped.

Holden lay sprawled on the living room carpet.

And blood was pooling under his head.

Chapter 18

As Damien had hoped when they'd left Gray to sit alone in his interrogation room for an hour, he was much more willing to talk and cut a deal than Ed had been. Gray had always been the softer of the two partners.

In fact, the man had cried through much of the interview.

"It was supposed to be some quick money! No one was supposed to get hurt. Just a few businesses put under."

Damien's teeth slammed together. "And what about the people who owned those businesses? Did you think of them?"

Gray swiped at his cheek. "They can start over somewhere else, you know? Insurance will cover the damage."

Damien met Case's gaze. *Unbelievable.*

Case nudged the digital recorder in the middle of the table a little closer to Gray. "Start at the beginning. How did you get involved in all this?"

Gray lifted a hand. "Ed came to me with the idea. You know that rich guy who just escaped jail?"

"Kirk Vossler. Yes."

"He and Ed grew up together back in Oklahoma. But they took different paths. And Vossler's wealth has always been a sticking point with Ed. He talked about it a lot. How he was suffering for making right choices all the time and how Vossler could help us get rich." Gray massaged the back of his neck. "I don't know. After a while it all started to sound pretty good, you know?" He fell silent staring at the tabletop.

"Go on," Damien urged.

"So when Ed came to me with this plan about how we could each make a hundred grand if we helped Vossler pull off a couple jobs, I gave in. I've got kids heading into their college years and nothing saved up." His voice broke.

Damien wasn't about to sympathize with the man. Case also held his silence.

"Well, when Vossler got pinched last year—"

"Wait," Damien interrupted. "This plan has been in place for over a year?"

Gray sighed, shoulders slumping under the weight of his guilt. "Yeah."

That would likely mean that Jack Kingston didn't know too much about this since he'd only been on the force for a little over six months and Miller's partner for only a couple weeks. Damien was relieved, though, of course, they would still need to check him out. He didn't know the kid well, but from what he'd seen, he had the makings of a good cop.

"Finish what you were saying," Case urged. "When Vossler got pinched..."

"He put this lady-friend of his in charge of continuing the plan."

"What's her name?" Case interjected.

Gray frowned in thought. "Kate... Dolly or Dolling?" He snapped his fingers. "Dollinger, I think. Something like that. She and Vossler had a kid together years ago. But then I think he got put up for adoption. I heard her mention it once. But we didn't talk to her much. She only came to a few of the planning meetings. The rest she attended on speaker phone. She lives out on one of the islands, I think." He waved a hand. "That's all I know."

"What was the plan?" Damien asked.

Gray's face sagged. "We paid a few people to start a peaceful protest. Then we paid a few more to instigate a riot."

Damien tensed. "Today's riots?"

"Yeah. We were supposed to get paid tonight after it all comes to an end."

Case jotted a few notes. "What was this supposed to accomplish?"

Gray traced a finger over the tabletop. "The riots were to happen only on certain blocks. Property values will go down. Vossler and his buddies will make money."

"His buddies?"

Gray sighed. "A couple of politicians. Two that people wouldn't suspect are working together because they come from different sides of the aisle."

Case plunked a pen onto the notepad in front of him and shoved it across the table to Gray. "You know the drill. We need all of this in writing. Every detail you can think of."

Gray's eyes were full of moisture again. "You're going to have to protect me. These people are ruthless."

Case rose, and Damien followed suit. "We'll get to work on that. You just write."

Outside the room, Case settled a hand on Damien's shoulder. "I'll get the warrants. You call Parker. He needs to hear about this woman who lives on the islands. He might know her."

Damien dialed Holden's number, but it rang clean through to voicemail. He left him a message. Then for good measure, fired off a text too.

He had that tremor of exhilaration in his gut. This investigation was finally coming together.

"Oh, dear Jesus." Camryn was still in the dining room. She covered her mouth. "Oh. Dear. Jesus!"

She couldn't move. All she could do was stare at Holden lying there partially hidden from her view.

And then Kate stepped through the door, gun pointed at her. "Don't worry. Everything is under control now."

"You killed him!" Camryn trembled from head to toe.

"Yes. But that's okay because it's fixed my problem. Well, at least part of it."

Momentarily speechless, Camryn could only stare at her.

"You see, when I killed Jay, I wasn't sure how I was going to cover it up. But this"—she swept a hand to indicate Holden—"provides it. Jay and Holden killed each other. Why they did so will always remain a mystery. Of course, there will always be those who question it." She rambled on, talking to herself, but Camryn was fixated on only a single thought.

Kate speaking to her this freely could only mean one thing. She was next.

"Yes, they've nicely fixed my problem. I'll only have to set up a few things." Kate suddenly quit talking, her gaze narrowing on Camryn. "But you, on the other hand, are still a problem." She waved the gun, pointing Camryn toward the back door. "Come on. We're going for a little walk."

Camryn fought through her shock. She'd better simply do as asked and pray for a way out to present itself. Since her own coat remained upstairs, she reached for the leather coat Holden had worn earlier, which hung on the rack. A sob caught in her throat as his cologne wafted to her.

"No," Kate snapped. "You won't be needing it anyhow." Her lips thinned into a chilly smile. "Out."

Camryn folded her arms against the biting wind as she stepped onto the back patio, as directed. "Why am I a problem?"

"Because I can't know what that nosy cop may have told you about the meeting he recorded. And because a lot of money is on the line. Not that trail," she barked when Camryn started to take the main path down the hill toward the clearing she was familiar with. "Keep walking. Through the woods there." She directed her toward the far end of the property.

Realization slammed into Camryn. The person in the shadows of that video must have been Kate.

"Move!"

Camryn trembled as she stepped off the patio and crossed the lawn toward the towering evergreens that edged the property. She let her gaze wander to the wondrous beauty stretched before her. Sometime in the past hour, another layer of fine snow had started to fall. The islands in the distance were gray mounds through a misty haze, and today the water had taken on a gray reflection of the sky. Was this to be her last view of earth?

Fitting, she supposed, that it should be of something dull and drab and gray. Because she was about to step through eternity's veil and into the most glorious sights and joys she'd ever experienced.

A wash of peace flooded her like she'd never experienced before, and she choked back a sob. Not a sob of terror for what was about to befall her, but a sob of sudden joy because she realized that she truly did believe. God had heard her prayer! She was awash, filled, flooded with belief!

In a few moments, she would step into heaven. And Holden, who had encouraged her so much in her faith, would be there to greet her. This time the sob that caught in her throat was one of sorrow mixed with joy. "Thank you, Jesus! I trust You. I believe."

"Stop that mumbling," Kate growled. "Go left. Through that brush there. Hurry up. I have to get back to the house and get Jay's body moved into position."

The sharp words jolted Camryn's focus from thoughts of heaven. And made her realize how biting the wind was. Her joints already ached with chill.

They were fully in the trees now, and she'd lost the view of the water except for brief glimpses of gray through the trees and thick underbrush.

Kate pushed her toward a once-used path overgrown by a thicket of salal. Icy water soaked into her clothes as she pushed through, and sharp leaves scratched her arms. The land sloped downward steeply.

"Keep going." Kate prodded her in the back with the barrel of the gun. "We're almost there. Faster."

Camryn folded her arms tight against herself. What had Holden's survival rules been again? Layers was the first rule, and Kate had deprived her of that.

She needed to distract herself from this misery. "Where are you taking me?"

"Someplace your body will never be found."

Camryn fought through the panic those words raised. *Lord, I need your strength. I do believe. Help me not to be scared.* More as an afterthought she tacked on, *Please, save me.*

The video recording she'd shown to Holden—had it been only a few minutes ago?—came to mind. And suddenly she wanted to fight back. She wanted to be there to attend Holden's memorial and see how his life had affected others like it had hers. Then she wanted to live a life of thankfulness and purpose because of his sacrifice for her. But no matter her wants, the chances of ever getting to do any of those things were slim. Still, if she was going to die, at least she could plant some doubts in the woman's mind about her continued safety. Maybe that would make her think twice before doing something like this again.

Camryn stepped over a thick tree root and pushed past her queasiness. "You were in the recording about the riots. The one with Soren Bane and Carter Cranston. Along with—"

"What do you know about that?" Kate grabbed her arm and yanked her around to face her.

For the first time, Camryn felt a measure of power over this woman. Not that it was going to get her anywhere. The Jumpdrive was still plugged into Holden's computer in the house. The thought of Holden sprawled on the carpet threatened to take her to her knees. But she had to think. Because it was her only leverage.

But what should she say about it? She could lie and say the recording had been sent to the authorities. It would be satisfying, even if fruitless. She brushed a lock of damp hair from her face. Despite the fact that they were under the trees, everything dripped and a fine mist penetrated bone deep. If she could just get warm, maybe she'd be able to think more clearly. She willed her teeth not to chatter. She didn't want to give Kate the satisfaction.

A niggling question lingered. "I don't understand why you killed Jay."

Kate leveled the gun at her head. "You tell me what you know about that recording, or I'll end you here and now."

Camryn swallowed and took a risk. "No. You won't. Because for some reason I don't understand, you don't want my body to be found. Why is that, anyhow?"

"Because if you are found here, that will link Holden's and Jay's deaths back to the events happening in Everett. And that can't happen. It could ruin everything."

A memory slammed through her mind. Jay in the kitchen, standing behind her with that big knife. "You wanted Jay to kill me, didn't you? You're linked to the death of that poor undercover officer. But how?"

Kate gritted a sound low in her throat. "Keep moving."

Camryn's boldness climbed another notch. "Not until you answer my questions. I doubt you want to drag the dead weight of my body all the way to this hiding place you've spoken about."

Kate swore. "If the deaths of the three officers are linked to the riots, it will build a fuel of resistance in all those business owners. For our plan to work, we need them to simply want to sell and move elsewhere. Buy low. Sell high. It's truly simple if you have all the right players and pay a few people to lead the mob."

Confirmation of what Holden had told her. These riots were all about money.

She glanced through the dripping trees, pondering what else she could do to delay the inevitable. "You never told me why you killed Jay."

"I killed him because he turned traitor. I birthed that boy! His allegiance should have been to me! But I overheard him on the phone. He planned to tell Holden all about me." Kate's eyes glittered. "He could have solved all our problems. I laid the plan out perfectly."

"What plan was that?"

"You ask a lot of questions. Shut up and move now, or I'll shoot you right here and roll your body down the hill into the water."

There was a glitter of truth in Kate's eyes this time, and Camryn believed her.

"Fine. I'm moving." With a shudder, she spun to face the trail once more. It was steep enough here that she couldn't keep her arms folded and maintain her balance, but at least if she walked, she'd keep her blood flowing—and maybe get to live for a few more minutes. She picked her way down the hill as slowly as she could without raising Kate's ire.

"He was supposed to kill you. Jay was. Then he was to make it look like someone had broken into the house and knocked him out, so when Holden got home, he would assume you'd been killed by the people he was trying to protect you from—which I suppose would have been true."

Camryn propped her hand against a trunk and navigated the tangled roots of another large evergreen. "I'm glad your son had more compassion and integrity than you do."

Kate huffed. "He was weak. Perhaps if I'd kept him all those years ago, I could have whipped some strength into him. Ahh! Here we are."

Camryn lifted her gaze from where she'd been concentrating on putting her feet to see that the steep hill of trees had given way to a rocky shore. A small cinder block platform peeped out from a cascade of blackberry brambles. To her horror, the ocean lapped right at the shoreline side of the structure. Ice encased the sides, but from here it looked like someone had built a large cinder-block deck over the water. It was built to hug the angle of the hillside that Camryn knew would continue beneath the surface of the water. It was likely that the waters here got deep almost immediately. The walls nearest them were only a few cinder blocks high, but out in the water, they rose ten or twelve feet to maintain a level. What was this place?

Wind gusted, tightening the gooseflesh on her dampened arms.

Kate gestured with the barrel of the gun. "Move the blackberries back right here."

Camryn pushed down nausea as she stepped forward, again only complying because it would delay the inevitable.

Most of the brambles sported tiny dangling icicles, but by this time her hands were so numb, cold was redundant. She tried to grasp the brush carefully, but with her numb fingers, her hands were clumsy. A thorn caught on her thumb and cinched a series of thorns into her palm. She cried out and yanked her hands back. Bloody scratches stretched the length of one palm.

She looked at Kate.

"I said move them!"

Camryn's gaze fell on a broken off tree branch. She lifted it and used it to push the remaining canes away from the structure. This revealed an inset into one wall part way down, with three stone steps that led down to a narrow metal door.

Kate nodded her head toward it. "Go."

Camryn eyed the water lapping only two feet away. Terror clawed at her throat. If the tide rose any higher, it would fill the well of the steps and likely flood the interior of whatever this strange building was.

The end of Kate's pistol thumped into the back of Camryn's head. "Move."

Camryn descended one step. Two steps. Three steps. She placed her hand on the door's old lever handle. Closed her eyes. Willed herself to strength. Whatever lay on the other side of this door, she knew the moment she stepped inside would be her last.

Chapter 19

Damien sat in the passenger seat as Case drove. His phone, which he'd shoved into his back pocket when he left his desk, was gouging into his hip. He tugged it free. The screen showed that he'd missed an email about an hour ago, but he didn't have time to look at it right now, so he simply shut off the screen and shoved the phone into the front pocket of his vest.

Gray's written statement had been enlightening.

Given the tenor of all that had happened in the world over the past few months, they hadn't had any trouble getting a conservative-leaning judge to give them a warrant for the arrest of not only Laurence Miller, but also Kirk Vossler, Kate Dollinger, and the two politicians. Gray had left Jack Kingston out of his statement altogether, and when they'd prodded him about the man, he'd said he didn't think Kingston was in on any of Miller's shady dealings. They'd have to bring him in for questioning to be sure, but Damien felt certain he would be cleared.

Gray hadn't known where Vossler was holed up, though he'd sworn up and down that it had to be nearby.

Ed still hadn't said a word after lawyering up.

But Damien had an idea that if Gray was right and Vossler was nearby, Miller might lead them to him. So instead of having Miller followed by some uniform who could potentially only be clocking in and clocking out, they'd taken on the detail themselves. Case had borrowed his wife's mid-sized gray sedan for the tail. And now they were trailing several blocks behind Miller's cruiser.

"I think he's slowing down." Case said.

Damien lifted the binoculars and studied the unit ahead. "He just pulled into that parking lot. He's getting out."

Case leaned forward and pointed up at the spinning neon pine-tree sign. "Evergreen Motel. What do you want to bet our jailbird found himself a tree to land in?"

Damien nodded. "And is getting visited by a snake."

"All right, then," Case said. "Let's do this."

Damien was already donning his bulletproof vest.

The high-pitched whine of a boat motor cut through the air. Camryn froze. From down in this door well, she couldn't see anything, but behind her on the top step, Kate swore.

"Get in there!" Kate jumped down the stairs and shoved her hard from behind, causing Camryn's body to crash into the door.

Since her hand was already on the door handle, it gave way beneath her weight, and she tried to catch herself as the door burst open.

Kate shoved her again, harder, panic chopping her breaths.

Camryn stumbled through the doorway, into a thick cloak of darkness.

Outside, the motor of the boat cut and someone hollered, "Kate? Was that you?"

Kate's vile words filled the black.

Camryn hunched her shoulders and tried to get her bearings. Willed her eyes to adjust to the darkness. Willed herself not to panic at the sound she heard—the sound of waves lapping and echoing in the hollow of a room.

"Kate Dollinger?" the voice from outside called again.

"Don't worry, Camryn. I'll be back for you in a moment." Kate pushed her and Camryn lurched forward. But where she'd expected her foot to meet the ground, there was nothing. Nothing but the ice-cold waters of the Salish Sea sweeping over her head.

It didn't take long for the motel's front desk employee, a blond, ponytailed kid with the scraggliest beard Damien had ever seen, to recognize Vossler and hand over the spare keys to his room.

"Is there a second way out of the room?" Case asked.

Ponytail shook his head.

"Windows? Even small ones?"

Another shake of his head. "The only windows in our units are on the parking lot side of the structure. The bathrooms are at the back and there are no windows or doors back there."

"How about a door into another room?"

"Not in his room."

"Thanks, kid."

They hurried down the walkway and, when they reached Vossler's door, Damien took one side and Case the other.

Damien waited, tense, gun drawn, and one shoulder planted into the wall, while Case spat on the key several times. It was a lubricating trick to make the key slide more silently into the doorknob.

Case lifted a brow at Damien.

Damien braced himself, gun at the ready, and gave him a nod. Adrenaline spiked through him, as it did every time he faced a situation like this. He could only offer up the briefest of prayers, as Case thrust the key home and turned the knob.

Damien burst into the room. "Police! Don't move!"

Vossler and Miller stood on the other side of a bed. Vossler was handing Miller an envelope. They spun toward the door, shock stretching their faces.

"Hands in the air!"

Miller dropped the envelope, hand sweeping toward his gun.

"Don't do it, Miller! Hands up!" Case barked from just behind and to Damien's left.

"All right, all right, all right!" Miller thrust his hands into the air. "Don't shoot."

Vossler froze for one second. And then he cursed Miller. "You led them right to me!" He lunged at Miller and came up with his gun.

Miller still had his hands raised. "Vossler, don't—"

Vossler shot him through the forehead.

Miller was still falling to the ground as Vossler swung the gun toward Damien.

Case and Damien both fired at the same time. Both bullets took the man through the chest. His shot went wild, and then the gun slipped from his hand and clattered into the corner of the room. His body hit the floor only seconds after Miller's.

Damien was breathing hard.

Case was too. His partner looked at him. "You hit?"

Damien assessed. "No. I'm good." He holstered his gun.

Case nodded, securing his own weapon. He advanced on the bodies and kicked Miller's gun farther from Vossler, even though it was clear from the man's wide, staring eyes he wouldn't be reaching for it again.

Damien bent and felt Miller's throat.

Case looked at him, waiting.

Damien shook his head. He dropped his gaze to the floor between his knees. He conjured up a memory of Sheila—the one of her batting her lashes at him as she licked frosting from her thumb. Her eyes twinkling with humor, her lips parting on a smile. He eased out a breath and came back to the scene.

Across the room, Case was already calling in the incident.

The paperwork on this would take hours. They'd have to give separate statements. But the bullet hole in the wall to the left of the door would make it pretty clear they'd been taking fire when they discharged their weapons. They would be cleared, but it would be a long night of waiting.

Tonight was supposed to be his date with Sheila. He wasn't going to make it.

He pulled out his phone to call her and noticed again on his lock screen that he had an email. This time the *from* name registered. Holden Parker.

He swiped to open it.

You'll want to watch this right away. Camryn found it in the pocket of her coat. She thinks Treyvon Johnson put it there. Holden

Damien's heart kicked up a beat. Could this be the information Treyvon had tried to get to him? The email contained a video link. He clicked it.

By fifteen seconds in, he was on his feet. "Case, you've got to watch this. We need to get it to the lab for enhancement, right away."

Camryn flailed. Fought through her terror. Tried to determine which way was up. The waves dragged her into deeper water, and she bobbed to the surface, but there was something hard above her head holding her under. She pounded at it, but, especially with the resistance of the water, her efforts were futile.

Her whole body was starting to go numb now, and a sharp pain pierced her skull. She'd been without oxygen for too long.

In that moment, instinct kicked in—literally. She kicked hard with her legs and stroked with her arms. Her feet pushed off something hard and she shot forward.

Her head burst above the water.

She treaded water and gasped a couple lungsful of oxygen. "Thank you, Jesus. Thank you, Jesus."

Her eyes were adjusted to the darkness now, and she could see that the inside of the cinderblock building was rimmed with a wooden deck shaped in a U. The open end of the U was in the deepest part of the water, and a garage-type door sealed off that end of the unit. She was in a boathouse. She swam to the nearest part of the deck and pulled herself out of the water.

Cold encased her in a glacial blanket. She wrapped her arms around herself and clamped her teeth against their chattering. She thought of Holden's rule number two. *Never get wet. Your chances of survival drop to near zero in that case.*

Outside she heard voices. She followed the boards back to the door and pressed her ear to it, willing herself to hear above the tremors wracking her body. It was no use. All she could make out was two female voices volleying through a conversation. She pulled back from the door and searched the room for any weapon. Because as soon as Kate had gotten rid of whoever was out there, she'd be back to finish what she'd started. But the room was empty. Nothing in sight except the rim of decking at her feet and the water filling the middle of the U.

Camryn eyed the garage door. Deep in the water, she could see a lighter strip that indicated the door didn't reach all the way to the ocean floor. She thought of the boat that had pulled up right outside to talk to Kate.

Holden had said not to get wet. But she was already wet. And near zero chances were better than her chances if she stayed in here and waited for Kate to come back for her.

But... she swallowed. She would have to go back in the water. Swim underwater, in fact. Under the door and all the way to the other side of the boat. Maybe she could use it to hide from Kate.

Before she could lose her nerve, she slipped off the deck and into the waves. She gasped at the shock of the icy waters but gave herself no time to adjust. The sooner she got out of here, the sooner she could get out of the water and figure out how to get warm. Taking a deep breath, she dove under. The boathouse doors only went about two feet under the waterline, leaving a good-sized gap for her to slip under.

Frigidity seemed to constrict every muscle, and the waves that had earlier pulled her into deep water now resisted her attempts to escape the boathouse. Panic stole her purpose and she bobbed back up inside. Tears threatened. But she couldn't give up.

She closed her eyes and pulled in a breath. "Jesus, give me peace. Give me strength. And warmth."

Outside, the boat engine roared to life. Kate called a loud goodbye.

This was her last chance!

The door banged open behind her.

With one last gulp of air, she willed herself silently beneath the black water, thankful it would take Kate's eyes a moment to adjust. This time, she remembered to use the proper underwater strokes. She kicked her legs firmly in tandem with firm sweeps of her arms and was through the gap!

But as she bobbed to the surface outside, the boat was already disappearing into the haze of falling sleet. Her hopes deflated. She was too late to catch it.

Behind her she heard a raucous round of cursing.

And then her leg spasmed into a cramp.

Chapter 20

A short dock extended from the side of the boathouse, with a ladder attached to the end. Fighting the cramp in her leg, Camryn dogpaddled to the ladder and hauled herself out of the water. Much as she would have liked to collapse on the boards of the dock, she didn't dare. Kate would emerge from the boathouse at any moment. She needed to get into hiding.

She hurried the length of the slush-slick dock and leapt from it onto the rocky shore. There was no beach here. Only land that gave sharply away to water. Her boot prints were clearly visible in the traitorous ice, but there was nothing she could do about that now. Maybe the falling sleet would fill them before Kate emerged.

Her boots gushed and slurped as she fought through thick shoreline brush toward Holden's clearing. The salal was thick. And the leaves had sharp points beneath the layer of wet slush that coated them. But her one aim was to put distance between her and Kate.

Her lips trembled with cold and every part of her ached.

She surged through one thicket, took a few steps, and encountered another.

Behind her the door of the boathouse clanged open.

Camryn collapsed into the center of the thicket, branches closing in above her head. She held her breath, listening. Not daring to move.

Kate cursed. "You can't escape me, Camryn! I know you're out here!" There was a pause, and then Kate gave a bellow of triumph.

She'd obviously found the footprints. Camryn's only hope now was to put as much distance between them as possible.

Camryn surged from her hiding place and sprinted as quickly as she could up the hill. The deeper into the trees she went, the less snow there would be. Also, that was in the direction of the house.

But Holden had told her to go to the cellar. She froze. She'd already ruined things by not listening to him once. Of course, his plan had been to come find her there, and that wouldn't happen now, but it *was* closer than the house. And it had bolts on the inside of the door. And a heater.

Behind her, Kate swore, crashing through the brush. "I was going to kill you quickly, Camryn. Now I'm changing my mind!"

Camryn changed directions and tore through a patch of salal in the direction of the cellar. The thicket clutched and tore at her and hindered every step, but she burst through the other side. And sobbed in relief. This was the familiar clearing. Now she only had to find the door.

She surged forward, but a tree root caught her boot, and her numb limbs were too slow to recover. She slammed into the ground, and another root glanced off the side of her head, shooting pain through her skull.

With a groan and a shake of her head, she pushed to her hands and knees and started to rise. But just then, Kate's feet came into view.

Camryn looked up.

Into the barrel of Kate's gun.

Kate was breathing hard, but Camryn was grudgingly impressed that a woman of her age had caught up to her so quickly.

She slumped onto the ground, all hope lost. She was beaten, shaking, scratched, and bloodied. "Just end it already."

Kate gave her a triumphant smile, still panting hard. "I will." She moved the gun to align with Camryn's head.

Camryn closed her eyes.

The shot came then, and Camryn flinched. Flinched? Had Kate missed? She braced for another shot, holding her breath.

Beside her something crashed into the brush.

Her eyes flew open. Kate no longer stood above her.

She scrambled away from where she'd fallen and rose to a crouch, spinning to search for what had crashed into the brush.

She gasped, hand flying to her mouth as she lurched backward.

Kate's body lay at an odd angle against a thicket of salal that had apparently repelled her fall. A trickle of blood dribbled down one of her cheeks. Her mouth hung open and her eyes stared sightlessly.

Footsteps crunched in the snow.

Camryn jolted and spun around to face the sound. Unbelieving, she blinked and blinked again. "H-Holden?"

He strode down the hill, stuffing a gun into the back of his waistband. One side of his head was still matted with blood. But his eyes! Oh! His eyes were full of life and fire that refused to let hers go.

She searched him from head to toe. "You're alive?"

His eyes crinkled. "I was just thinking the same about you."

"I can't believe it."

One corner of his mouth ticked up as he stopped before her. "Takes more than mere bullets or crazed gun-wielding women to take us superheroes down."

She wanted to laugh, but part of her still couldn't believe what had just happened. She dragged her gaze to Kate. And then the trembling set in. Tears blurred her vision, and the shaking in her limbs grew so strong that she stumbled.

"Come here. I've got you. Don't look at her." Holden wrapped his arms around her and pulled her to him. He turned her head away from the sight of Kate and hugged her briefly, but then he set her back from him and shrugged out of his leather coat, swinging it around her shoulders. He pulled her back against his chest, and the warmth of the coat enveloped her in a cocoon of his scent. She tucked her face into the collar and simply relished the sturdy strength of him supporting her weight.

After a moment, the wind picked up, slicing through the wet fabric of her jeans and reminding her she was still soaking wet.

She lifted her face to Holden's. "I'm sorry I let Kate see me at your house."

He crooked one finger under her chin and caressed her with his thumb, shaking his head. "She knew anyhow, remember? She'd seen your packages already."

Camryn studied the center of his T-shirt. "That was my fault too. I should have changed the name on the address."

His thumb continued to tantalize her chin. "If we are going to cast blame, I should have thought to tell you to put my name on the packages. But neither of us knew Kate would go so far as to snoop through my mail in her suspicion."

Camryn searched his face. "I'm so glad you're alive. When I saw all that blood under your head, I thought…" Tears filled her vision and choked off her voice.

Holden cupped her face and swiped her tears with his thumbs. "She only clipped me a good one along the side of the head. See?" He angled his head.

The gash was shallow, and it seemed to have stopped bleeding, even if his hair was still matted with blood.

Camryn reached a hand toward it but couldn't bring herself to go farther than touching his cheek. "You should get that checked out at a hospital."

He turned his face into her palm and dropped a kiss there. "I will. But first I have to tell you I'm very disappointed in you."

The teasing note in his voice lightened the mood, but she had no idea what he could be talking about. She tilted her head and searched his face. "Oh?"

He nodded. "You broke one of my cardinal rules about cold survival. You got wet."

She chuckled. "I did. But in my defense, I was pushed. She took me to some boathouse over there." She pointed.

"My neighbor's. His father was an avid boater, but he's too busy with work to use it. If Kate had succeeded..." He didn't seem able to complete the sentence. Instead, he cupped a hand at the side of her head and dropped a kiss into her hair. "I'm sorry I didn't do a better job of protecting you. I missed all the signs."

Camryn laid a finger to his lips. "She was just an eccentric old woman. The perfect disguise. I don't blame you. Not at all." And since the conversation needed to return to a lighter tone, she quirked him a smile. "And I want you to know that I really am a superhero because I had to swim to get away."

His brows arched. "I'm impressed. You'll have to tell me all about it, but first I want to get you out of this cold. Think you can walk?"

She nodded, but on her first step, her numb foot twisted beneath her.

"Whoa, there!" Holden swept her into his arms and started up the hill.

She wrapped her arms around his neck, embarrassed to be so helpless. "I'm sorry."

"I'm not." He winked at her.

Chapter 21

Three weeks later.

Camryn had unpacked the last box of things she'd brought with her from the mainland and set the last book on the small bookshelf in her upstairs ocean-view room. She stepped back and looked around in satisfaction.

The view from the room's large octagonal window was gorgeous, and never before in her life had she been more aware of how God's guiding hand had directed her to this place. If she hadn't been walking that Everett street that fateful night, she never would have ended up here. Thankfulness for a loving God who'd directed her even when she wasn't aware of it, swept through her.

Mrs. Hutchinson was thrilled to have her renting this room, and already Camryn had eaten more baked goods than she probably did all last year. She would have to come up with a workout schedule, or she was going to bloat up like one of the whales that could sometimes be seen from her window.

"Yoo-hoo!" Mrs. Hutchinson called up the stairs to her. "The sheriff is here. And he's asking to see you!"

Camryn's heart rate ratcheted up a notch. The elderly woman made it sound like he was here to call, but Camryn glanced at her phone. Sure enough, it was time for Holden to pick her up for her first day of work.

"Coming!" she called.

A vehicle would need to be the next thing on her "to buy" list.

She grabbed the suit jacket she'd chosen for today and reassessed herself in the mirror on the back of her door. She patted her upswept hair and gave her business attire a nod. She would do.

She hurried down the stairs to meet Holden. Excitement at the prospect of seeing him had her stomach quavering. It had been a whole week since she'd seen him last.

On doctor's orders, he'd been at home on bed rest this past week. It had taken her two weeks after the shooting to talk him into going to get his head checked. And just as she'd suspected from his constant headaches, he'd sustained a fracture when Kate shot him. Thankfully, it had only been what the doctor had called a "simple linear fracture." But the doctor had mandated that he rest, flat on his back for a week.

Holden had been none too happy about it. And Camryn hadn't felt comfortable enough in their relationship to go to his house to visit him.

During the first week after the shooting, she'd seen him often due to the investigation into Kate's death. While they'd never been able to enhance the video Camryn had found enough to definitively say that Kate had been in the warehouse meeting, they'd found plenty of evidence at her house to indicate she'd been one of the ringleaders planning the riots. They'd also found on her computer the video the kid in the GTO had taken of Camryn the night of the hit and run, and a grainy picture of Camryn sitting on the street, obviously taken by someone else. Camryn still shivered when she thought about that.

Unfortunately, that first day, they'd also found Jay's body in the passenger seat of his car. Kate had killed him. And the officers from Everett had confirmed that he was indeed her son—hers and Kirk Vossler's. They'd apparently been together years ago and recently rekindled their relationship.

The detectives seemed to think Kate might have been using Vossler for his money because they'd found evidence at her house of a plan to eliminate him once he'd set her up with the cheaply purchased real estate and businesses.

The two politicians who'd also been in the warehouse video had been arrested and were slated to stand in separate trials early next month.

From the stairs, Camryn noted Holden pacing in Mrs. Hutchinson's living room. She paused on the bottom step, taking him in. In his brown uniform, with his Stetson in one hand, he looked wonderful and handsome and...grumpy?

Her heart rate stuttered. She'd hoped he'd be as excited to see her as she was to see him. "Hi," she ventured uncertainly.

He spun to face her, his leisurely gaze drifting the length of her. His throat worked. "Hi, yourself."

"How are you feeling?"

A sweep of his hat brushed away her concern. "Fine. Tired of laying around."

She let her gaze skim his uniform. "I see that you are planning to get right back to work."

His fingers crimped the brim of the hat. "No reason not to. You ready?" He looked toward the door.

Her disappointment mounted. "Yes."

Bluebell hissed at Camryn as she came off the last step. She gave the cat a wide berth, having learned after her first day not to try to make friends with the grumpy, entitled feline.

Holden was still frowning. In fact, his face right now could give Miss Bluebell a run for her money. Camryn hid a brief smirk as she thrust her arms into her jacket.

But then, once more, she acknowledged her disappointment. What had put the sour in his cream? Since they hadn't seen each other for a week, she'd expected this reunion to be a joyful one.

He swept open the front door and held it for her.

"Bye," Mrs. Hutchinson called. "I'll have dinner waiting when you get home."

"Thank you!" Despite her disappointment with Holden's greeting, Camryn took the sidewalk with a light step. She was looking forward to her first day on the job, and she wasn't even afraid to admit that it was mostly because she would get to spend the day with one handsome, currently grumpy boss.

He swept open the cruiser door but then touched her shoulder before she could get in. "Listen, Camryn. There's something I need to clear up before we get started. We're going to be working together and"—his finger swung back and forth between them—"we can't... There can't be anything between us in a situation like that. Are you following me?"

She felt her expression fade and folded her arms in a protective shield. "I see... I understand. It will be fine."

His brow furrowed. "Yeah."

She searched his face. He looked like he was in pain. "How is your head?"

He waved a hand. Looked away. "Fine. A lot better, actually." His gaze flicked back to hers. "I thought you might come by the house to see me."

She refused the little buds of hope that poked through the soil of her heart. "I wanted to give you the time to rest like the doctor said. I used the week to finalize moving out of my Everett apartment and into my room here."

He made a noncommittal noise. He swept his hat to indicate she should get in. "Guess we should get going."

Hurt by his continued rejection, she snipped, "Yes. I guess we should." She turned to climb into the vehicle.

Behind her, he growled. "Hang it, Cam." His fingers wrapped around her arm and he tugged her to him. He held her close with one hand at the small of her back, while his other arm crooked along the top of the door and curved around her head. "What am I going to do with you?"

She held her breath. Searched his face. Didn't dare to hope.

His thumb swept over her hair. "You're going to be in my office every day looking cute, beautiful, gorgeous—and every increment in between. And every time I pass by your desk, I'm going to think about kissing you. Like I'm doing right now."

She felt her eyes grow wide. "I'm getting mixed signals here, Holden."

He gave a short grunt. "Unfortunately, my signals aren't mixed at all. They are all clearly shouting one thing." His head dipped, and his lips hovered above hers just long enough to give her the chance to escape, before they settled against hers, soft, searching, supple.

With a moan Camryn melded into him, giving as good as she got. His hand at her back tugged her closer, and his other caressed the tumble of hair that was now cascading down her back.

A fleeting thought registered. She was going to have to redo her hair, but she didn't care.

Her lips gave way pliantly to his. She fit perfectly against the strength of him. Her hands curled around his face.

After a moment, he stepped back, pressing the pad of his thumb over his lips. "Wow, woman."

She stared at him, eyes wide, chest rising and falling on rapid breaths. "Wow yourself." She reached to gather her hair. "So..." She winced. "Am I fired before my first day has even begun?"

He sighed and plopped his hands on his hips. His gaze swept her. "Do you think you could show up for work looking a little less appealing?"

Camryn smiled at him as she finished clipping up her hair. Then she stepped right to him and slipped her palms across his chest. She gave him a coy bat of her lashes. "Maybe you could loan me those old baggy sweats and that Seahawks jersey."

He snorted. "Not on your life. The moment I saw you come down the stairs in those I knew I was a goner."

She giggled. Felt her face heat. Standing on tiptoe, she pressed her lips to his, lingering over the task. After a long moment, she eased back. She glanced at him through her lashes. "So what *would* you like me to wear?"

His eyes twinkled, and humor softened his features. "Maybe you could come to work wearing one of those hazmat suits? You know the ones with the full head gear that make it look like you're about to step down for a moon landing?"

She pursed her lips and frowned. "Hmmm... That might make typing and answering phones slightly difficult. What about one of those orange prison jumpsuits? Would that do?"

He laughed and pulled her to him. "Don't you dare."

Her brows shot up. "Oh! A dare!"

He swooped in for another lingering kiss.

With her arms looped behind his neck, she looked up at him. "So I'm not fired for fraternizing with my boss?"

He chuckled and bopped her on the nose. "Your boss says no. We can figure this out."

She quirked him a look. "Is your pendulum done swinging now? Because I can't go through this every day."

He smiled. "Sorry to put you through the wringer. I'm decided now. We'll make it work."

"Well, all right, then. Let's get to the office."

"Yeah, we probably should do that." He took her hand to help her into the cab of the cruiser.

From behind them, they heard a chuckle. They both turned to find Mr. Snowden standing in a thick, ratty, blue-and-gray bathrobe that looked like it might have gotten caught in a lawn mower a time or two. It was probably two sizes too large for him. He grinned at them from his side of the box hedge. His dog Periwinkle stood on back legs with paws propped on the hedge next to his owner, also watching them.

Mr. Snowden swiped a hand of dismissal and grinned. "Don't mind us. We're just getting in our morning stretch."

Holden lifted the man a wave.

A tapping sound drew their gazes to the house.

Mrs. Hutchinson waggled her fingers at them, eyebrows pumping.

Holden huffed out a chuckle.

Camryn grinned up at him as he finished helping her into the cab. "Maybe I could borrow Mr. Snowden's robe to wear over your sweats and jersey. Would that work?"

He threw back his head on a laugh. And was still laughing by the time he got into the driver's seat. He reached over and took her hand. "Let's get to work."

Sheer satisfaction filled Camryn's heart. For the first time in a long time she felt like she had truly come home. "Yes. Let's."

Also available...

The Unrelenting Tide

You may read an excerpt on the next page...

John 15:12-13

This is my command:
Love one another the way I loved you.
This is the very best way to love.
Put your life on the line for your friends.

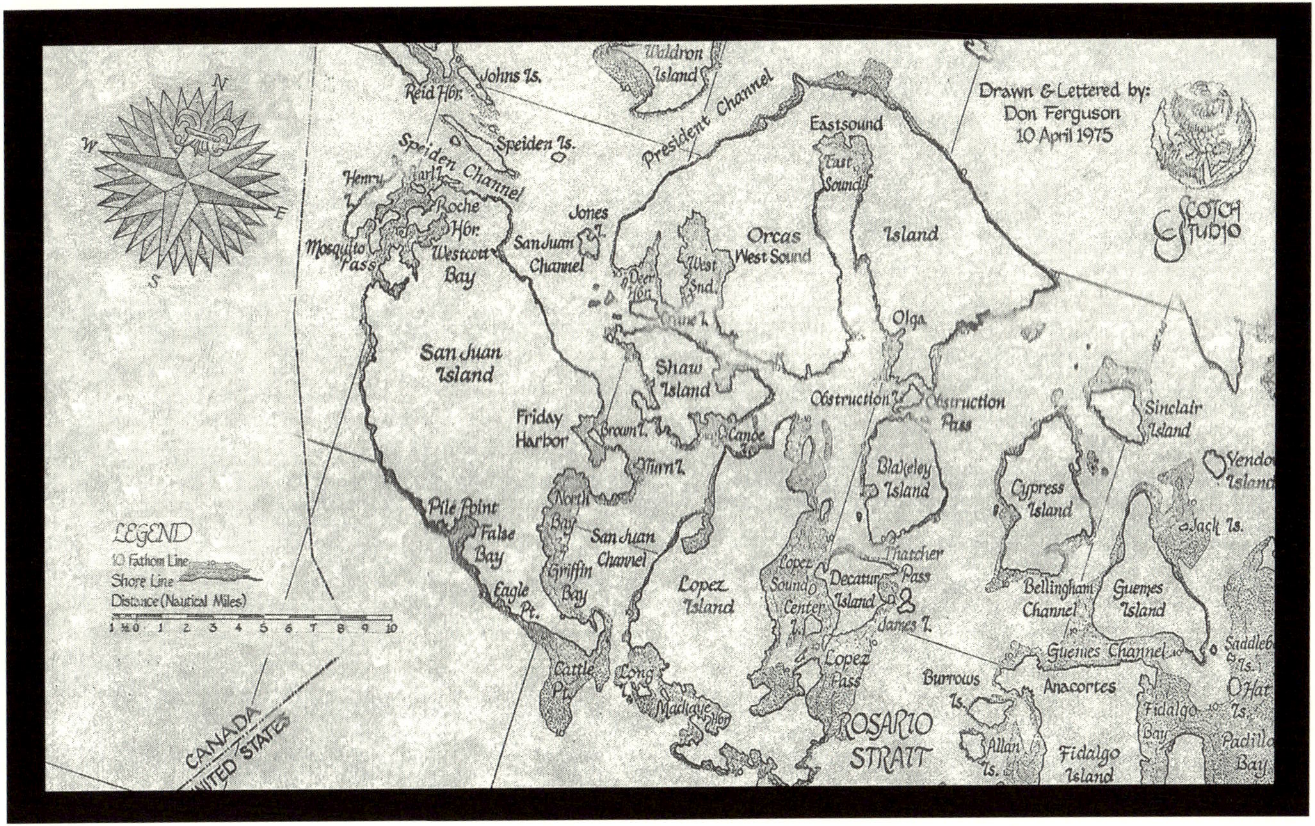
Drawn & Lettered by:
Don Ferguson
10 April 1975
Scotch Studio
N
E
S
W
LEGEND
10 Fathom Line
Shore Line
Distance (Nautical Miles)
1 ½ 0 1 2 3 4 5 6 7 8 9 10
Waldron Island
Johns Is.
Reid Hbr.
Speiden Is.
Speiden Channel
President Channel
Henry I.
Roche Hbr.
Mosquito Pass
Westcott Bay
Jones I.
San Juan Channel
San Juan Island
Friday Harbor
Brown I.
Turn I.
Pile Point
False Bay
Eagle Pt.
Cattle Pt.
North Bay
San Juan Channel
Griffin Bay
Eastsound
East Sound
Orcas
West Sound
Island
West Snd.
Deer Hbr.
Crane I.
Olga
Shaw Island
Canoe I.
Obstruction I.
Obstruction Pass
Blakeley Island
Thatcher Pass
Decatur Island
James I.
Lopez Sound
Center I.
Lopez Island
Lopez Pass
Long
Mackaye Hbr.
ROSARIO STRAIT
Burrows Is.
Allan Is.
Sinclair Island
Cypress Island
Vendovi Island
Jack Is.
Bellingham Channel
Guemes Island
Guemes Channel
Anacortes
Fidalgo Island
Fidalgo Bay
Saddlebag Is.
Hat Is.
Padilla Bay
CANADA
UNITED STATES

Chapter 1

A scream gargled at the back of Devynne Lang's throat, jolting her from terrorized slumber. With a whimper she kicked back covers tangled against damp legs, yanked open the nightstand drawer, and fumbled for the familiar feel of her .38 special.

The rubberized, laser-trigger grip felt cool against her palm. She gave a firm squeeze. The red laser light pierced the darkness beside the balcony curtains. Through the bathroom door. Into the black maw of her closet. Her gaze jerked from corner to corner, scrutinizing each shadow, each waver of light.

Nothing.

Her own ragged breathing registered and she blinked slowly. Pulled in a long full inhale, then released it along with some tension.

No one was here. It was the nightmare.

Again.

Running a hand back through her hair, she glanced down. She knelt in the middle of her bed, t-shirt and shorts plastered with sweat, knees denting sheets so jumbled it seemed a wrestling match had taken place. The angry red numbers of the clock on the nightstand read 4:30am.

If Marissa stayed true to form she would be up in a couple of hours begging to watch *Nickelodeon* while she ate her breakfast.

Devynne sank back against her ankles. Best she get on with her day. She took one more calming breath, then forced her legs over the edge of the bed.

Pulling back the floor length curtains, she peered out onto the deck and gave the slider a tug to make sure it was still locked. The faint gleam of morning, just beginning to peek above the islands across the way, tinged the water gray and outlined the evergreen trees in the back yard stark black against the sky. All was as it should be.

Still, to be safe, she padded across the hall and checked Marissa's room. No one behind the door. No one in the closet – the light was still on, just as she'd left it the night before when she tucked Marissa in. The only sound was the soft sonorous breaths the four-year-old made from under her Disney princess blanket on the canopied bed.

She crept down the stairs from the top level of her tri-story. Checked the kitchen, guest bath, living room, and the deck's sliding door in the same way she'd done upstairs. No one on the middle level and the back door in the kitchen was still locked too.

A quick flip of the light switch in the sewing room on the bottom floor, revealed it was also empty. The slider to its deck also remained locked.

Relief eased a little more of the strain – what she needed now was a hot shower to wash away the last vestiges.

Back in her room, she returned the Smith & Wesson Airweight to the nightstand, locked the drawer and took the key into the bathroom with her, hanging it high on the corner of the mirror like she did every morning.

She slapped on the hot water and let it run as she thought over her day.

Carcen was coming this morning to take Marissa to his team's summer basketball game. He had mentioned the game several times this week and she knew he was a bit nervous for the varsity boys he coached, even though he wouldn't have admitted it for anything.

Devynne pulled the shower curtain shut and stepped under the hot spray.

She would need to get Mrs. Abernathy's quilt finished soon. She'd better concentrate on that one today. One little misstep on that project and Mrs. Abernathy would be sure to let the world know what a disaster her dealings with *The Healing*

Quilt had been. Devynne couldn't afford the bad publicity. The company she'd started after her husband's death four years previous, had been her only means of support since.

The Seattle Quilters' Guild had called yesterday and left a message to see if she could machine quilt three king size, a queen, and two double quilts in the next couple weeks.

Thank you God for the extra work. The bills had been piling up for awhile now.

She rinsed the shampoo out of her hair and thought of the account she hadn't touched since she'd fled California six years ago. How much money would be in it now?

Don't go there.

Marissa's safety was too important to ever go back for that money. Shania Hane, up-and-coming actress, had died on a cold February day six years ago – at least that was the story she'd paid her agent to tell – and Shania Hane needed to remain dead.

For now.

Marissa would need a good college education someday. Maybe then they would go back for the money. Maybe.

For now, it was too dangerous.

So, even though it would mean several late nights over the days to come, she would call the guild today and agree to take on the extra pieces.

She cranked the shower head to the massage setting and rolled her neck through the pounding water letting it beat away the last of the tension and adrenaline. She could have stood there all day, but the scent of freshly brewed coffee from her programmable pot lured her back to reality, and she shut off the tap.

The towel soft against her skin, she dried off, wrapped up, and stepped out into her room to grab her jeans and a t-shirt.

She froze.

Her night stand drawer stood cracked open, the key hanging from the lock in the front face.

The room's lights were on now. A quick scan proved she was alone. Hadn't she just put her gun in there, locked it, and hung the key in the bathroom?

Marissa!

She rushed to the drawer half expecting to find it empty, but the gun lay right where she always left it. Hurrying to snatch it up, she knocked it against the drawer. It tumbled from her grasp and landed on her foot.

She grunted as pain sliced across her arch, but grabbed it up again and raced across the hallway to Marissa's room, checking the loads as she went. All chambers held rounds.

Heart thudding so hard she could feel the beat of it as she clutched the towel close, she pushed open Marissa's door with one foot and stepped into the room, gun at the ready.

Nothing ahead. Nothing left, or right. The closet light still cast golden illumination across the Sleeping Beauty castle-shaped rug. Deep, undisturbed breathing still resonated.

Devynne slumped against the wall and leaned her head back. *Thank you, Jesus!*

Just that quickly she resumed her vigil. Someone could still be here!

No one was under the bed – she'd purposely gotten Marissa a high bed, and insisted she not store any toys underneath for times just like this – and the morning light streaming in from the window gleamed unbroken beneath it now. There was nowhere else to hide.

No one was here. *Please God, let that be true.*

A quick check through the rest of the levels, each deck, window, and door, revealed she and Marissa were the only ones in the house. And everything was still locked up.

Back in her room, she collapsed onto the edge of the bed and scooped damp hair away from her face with a trembling hand.

She was losing her mind.

She glanced down at the nightstand. There was no explanation other than she'd only *thought* she put the gun away and locked the drawer.

If Marissa had woken while she was in the shower and found the gun...

Her whole body shook at that thought. How could she have been so careless?

Tears pricked her eyes and exhaustion washed over her. She wanted nothing more than to flop over, pull the covers up to her neck, and not get up for another eight hours. The unending string of long days and late nights had been weighing heavy for the past few weeks.

She blinked hard. *Get a grip!*

She could do this. She *had* to do this. A little girl across the hall needed her mommy to be strong, keep her fed, and keep a roof over her head. And Mommy wasn't going to let her down. Not in a million years.

She laid the gun back into the drawer. Shut it and locked it. Tested the drawer to make sure it wouldn't open. Then pulled on it one more time, for good measure. Satisfied that she had indeed locked the gun away this time, she stood.

Pain knifed through her right foot. She gasped and looked down.

A gash across the top of her foot seeped blood.

She grimaced. *Great start to the day, Devynne. Just great.*

CHAPTER 2

The growl of Carcen's truck out in the driveway grated in dissonant contrast to the purr of her sewing machine. So he'd arrived. Good. She'd felt jittery and tense all morning – getting up every ten minutes to check on Marissa, double check that they were alone in the house, and verify that the doors were still locked. Maybe now, with Marissa off at the game with Carcen's parents she would be able to get some work done.

"Rissa! Uncle Carcen's here to take you to the game!"

"Yay!" The thunder of small feet pounded down the stairs from the top floor.

"Don't open the door till I get there!" Sighing, Devynne threw the quilt piece she was working on over her shoulder and stood. Pain flamed through her foot and she snatched a breath. She'd been using it on the sewing machine pedal, but apparently standing on it was a different matter altogether. Gritting her teeth and forcing herself to walk as normally as possible, she made her way up to the middle level.

She stopped at the top of the stairwell just in time to see Marissa launch herself into the arms of her uncle, who had just stepped through the kitchen door. Her heart gave an extra thump and she reminded herself to batten down her emotions.

But as she watched Carcen blow a raspberry against Marissa's neck, she cringed and aggravation with her daughter washed through her. She leaned a shoulder into one wall. What if it hadn't been Carcen? She should have come upstairs quicker and made Marissa wait until she was a hundred percent certain it was Carcen at the door. In their small community Marissa had a bad habit of throwing the door open to whoever rang the bell. She'd talked to her about it a hundred times, but it looked like she'd have to talk with her again.

Carcen bumped the door shut with his foot and swung the four-year-old around and around.

Marissa clung to him tightly, giggling all the while, her dark curls swirling about her face.

When Carcen finally stopped his dizzying twirl, the little girl gazed up into his face, her large, brown eyes wide with excitement. "Do it 'gain, Uncle Cawce. Do it 'gain."

Carcen threw back his head on a laugh.

Devynne's heart squeezed and gave a double-thump that she did her best to ignore. Carcen was so much like Kent had been, yet so different at the same time. The same lithe, athletic form. The same sense of fun-loving humor. The same curls, but blond more than brown. When would the sight of him quit bringing pain? And when had it started making her wonder what it might be like to be in a man's arms again? Her face heated and she was glad all his attention was focused on her four-year-old.

Now he gaped down at Marissa. "Do it again?!" Hugging her close to his chest, he staggered past Devynne into the living room, pretending to be drop-down-dizzy, the little pixy swaying crazily in his arms. "I can't even walk straight!"

"Yo' silly, Uncle Cawce." Marissa cupped his stubbled cheeks in her tiny hands and looked him right in the eye. "Are you weally gonna play the meanest team in the lake?"

He chuckled, a deep rumble from his chest, and glanced over at her as he set Marissa on her feet.

Devynne suppressed her own humor, remembering that when he had called to ask if Marissa could accompany him and his parents to the basketball game he had emphasized to Marissa that she would have a great time watching his team pulverize the 'meanest team in the league'.

"League, honey, not lake." Devynne stepped fully into the living room and smoothed the girl's curls as she spoke. "A league is a group of teams that play against each other. And what have I told you about opening the door?"

Marissa hung her head. "I pulled back the cuwtain and see'd it was Uncle Cawce befowe I opened it."

Carcen nodded his agreement to that statement.

She sighed. "Well, if you're going to watch Uncle Carcen's team play the meanest team in the *league* you'd better go get your shoes on."

Wide eyed, the little girl rounded her mouth in a silent 'oh' as she glanced mischievously down at her wiggling toes. Peeking up at her uncle through her bangs, she rolled her eyes as if to say 'oh my goodness she's right' and quickly whirled, racing to the third floor without a word.

Carcen turned the full force of his breath-stopping-blues on Devynne, his face suddenly turning serious. He shoved his hands deep into the pockets of his slacks, his purple Friday Harbor High School polo stretching taut across his shoulders. "How are you?"

"Fine." A noose of dread cinched around her chest and she met his gaze for only a second before she looked down, knowing what his next question would be.

"Why don't you come with us?"

She smiled placatingly, answer ready. "I can't this time. I have this quilt I need to finish for Mrs. Abernathy's new cabin." She gestured to the piece on her shoulder. "It's the last one she ordered and I have to have it done soon. Maybe another time."

Her gaze flickered to his for a scant second, yet in that brief moment she saw the truth on his face. He knew. She started up the stairwell. "I'll go make sure her shoes get on the right feet."

She just couldn't bring herself to go out. The old fears always rode her hard. Always the feel of someone watching her. And that didn't even take into consideration the guilt over Kent's death, which most likely had been her fault.

She sighed as she trudged up the tan, carpeted treads, trying not to limp even as pain throbbed.

Grandma used to say trouble came in packs. So true. Hers had been rolling in, one wave after another, for the last seven years. An unrelenting tide of pain and misery.

She knew for Marissa's sake she probably needed to get out more. But when it came to getting back into the swing of life it was simply easier, and safer, to keep to herself. After that terrible day at Island Grocers she had felt guilty - somehow unfaithful - going out and enjoying herself when Kent wasn't around to enjoy life with her. Now, she dreaded the looks of pity and curiosity she was sure to get from everyone. Things were easier when she kept to herself. Not to mention diminishing the likelihood that someone might recognize her.

She had joy enough right here at home.

Even now, she smiled as she eased the weight off her foot and leaned in her daughter's doorway, watching her try to fasten her sandals.

Tongue caught between her teeth, little face scrunched up into a mask of concentration, she attempted to thread the small metal clasp into the correct hole, then rolled her eyes in frustration. Never mind that the shoe was already on the wrong foot.

Devynne knelt before her. "Here look. This shoe goes on the other foot. See the toe of the shoe? Your big toe goes here at this pointier part. Let Mom help you so you won't keep Uncle Carcen waiting."

Marissa pushed herself to her feet and scampered over to sit in Devynne's lap. She held up one pudgy foot at a time and Devynne worked the shoes over stubborn heels and fastened the clasps. Shoes on, the tyke turned and hugged her tight. "I wuv you, Mama. Want to come?"

Devynne smiled softly, but she suddenly sensed Carcen in the doorway behind them. She glanced over her shoulder.

He leaned there, arms folded, a slight frown puckering his brow.

How was it he always walked with stealthy, cat-like silence? She rarely heard him approach, but could always seem to sense when he was there. Right now she could feel the disapproval rolling off him in waves. He had voiced, on more than one occasion, his opinion that she should quit feeling sorry for herself and start living again.

She sighed, turning back to Marissa. Maybe he had a point. But... *If he knew the whole story he'd likely feel differently.*

Stroking the child's hair, she shook her head. "I can't this time, Honey. You go and have fun with Uncle Carcen. You don't get to see his boys play ball very often. And be good for Grandma and Grandpa, OK?"

Marissa's lower lip protruded and she hung her head down until her chin touched her chest.

"Honey—"

Carcen cut her off. "Hey, none of that. If you are coming with me, we can't have your lip hanging out. Especially not so far. My star player might trip on it while he's dribbling down the court. Then the meanest team in the lake might beat us."

A solitary giggle escaped as Marissa glanced up at hzer uncle. "The *league*, Uncle Cawcen, not lake!"

"Oh! Right!" He tossed her a wink. "Why don't you go down and wait for me by the door. I left my coat on the table and you might even find a piece of gum in my pocket."

Marissa was gone in a flash and Devynne climbed wearily to her feet. On the pretense of cleaning up the room, she began to gather some of the clothes scattered about, keeping her back to him and hoping he would just go this time without making a big deal of her not coming. But she could feel his gaze drilling her from behind. She moved to pick up a sock in the far corner then paused to straighten the pieces to the doll house Marissa had been playing with all morning.

"If you just ignore me long enough I'll have to go away, is that it?" His voice was a low growl but she heard the concern around the edges.

The concern was almost her undoing. Devynne pinched the bridge of her nose, willing herself not to allow the tears until he left. "Don't do this Carcen. I *can't* come. I have *work* to do. Maybe next time."

"That's what you've said for the past several years, Devynne." His tone dropped to a soft murmur touched with disheartenment.

She swallowed hard and pushed strength into her knees. "Yeah? Well, for the past several years I've been trying to make a *living* for Marissa and I. I've been busy."

"What happened to your foot? You're limping."

She tensed. No way could she tell Sheriff Carcen Lang she'd thought there was an intruder in the house and in her panic had dropped her gun on her bare foot. Her heart gave an extra thump and she reminded herself to hoist up her self-control. If he even had a hint of what her morning had been like he would morph into cop-mode faster than his star player could sink a three-pointer.

"I dropped something on it." She waved a hand to indicate it was no big deal and prayed he'd just let it go.

Carcen hesitated. She hadn't hidden her tears as well as she probably thought she had. But he needed to get going.

He folded his arms, unfolded them, glanced at his watch, and then folded them again. Stubborn woman. How was he ever going to get through to her? He just wanted her to be happy again. "I have to go." Reaching out he pulled the pink Barbie pajamas off the end of Marissa's bed, tucking them under his arm. "I'll be back later this evening."

Her back still to him, Devynne nodded. "OK. See you then."

He knew her well enough to detect the note of relief edging her voice.

She could be relieved for now. But come tonight they were going to have this out, once and for all.

CHAPTER 3

Devynne stayed at her sewing machine all through the afternoon and well into the dinner hour before a headache made her realize she hadn't eaten anything since her coffee and toast that morning.

Stretching, she surveyed her day's work. Most of the quilt top was assembled. She just needed to add one border and then do the binding. And it was beautiful. Even Mrs. Abernathy would be hard pressed to find something to complain about on this quilt.

Satisfaction eased through her. Despite the woman's grumpiness, she was quite influential. A good word from her and Devynne could expect several more orders from the woman's bridge club friends.

As Devynne took the stairs up to the kitchen, her foot pulsed pain with each step. But the further she went the less it hurt. Maybe she should take a little walk to work out the kinks from tightened muscles.

In the kitchen she assembled a sandwich and grabbed an apple from the bowl on the counter. Slipping into her Mary Jane water shoes, and grabbing up her keys, she stepped out onto the midlevel deck and locked the door behind her. The rest of the house was already locked up – she'd made sure after Carcen left with Marissa.

Taking a big bite of ham and pickles on whole-wheat, she paused to stare out over the Salish Sea. The day couldn't be more beautiful. Through the softly swaying branches of the evergreen trees in her back yard, the sun glinted off the calm lazuline water below. Both Shaw and Orcas Island were plainly visible, dark green against the lighter backdrop of the sky.

From where she stood, she could have tossed a pebble and it would have landed in the water. Below her the waves teased at the shoreline, their soft rhythm a soothing symphony against the counterpoint of birdsong and rustling wind.

The stairs at the side of the deck led down to the side yard where a sloping path extended down to the lowest level of the yard. She took the stairs and the path slowly, savoring the sun warming her shoulders, and the breeze taking the edge off the heat. Far out in the water a black and white orca crested and blew a geyser into the air, then disappeared with a slap of its tail. Near her on the path a squirrel chattered and she tossed him the last corner of her crust. He cocked his head, angling her a cautious look before darting out to snap up the scrap and scamper back to safety.

A sigh eased from her lips and she sank down onto the wooden, half-log bench Kent had built in the back yard. She closed her eyes tipping her head back to relish the breeze's caress, the constant slapping of the waves against the floating dock, the cry of a gull. She searched for the bird and found it, wings spread wide, cavorting with the currents of air high overhead. Off to her right the familiar green and white *Evergreen State* ferried by, her decks high off the water. *Must not have too many riding the inter-island route today.*

Some of Devynne's tension eased. She and Marissa really should have moved to a smaller place by now. Or at least rented out the big house and moved into the small guest house at the back of the property. But this, this little taste of heaven and privacy, she could never seem to let it go. Five minutes down here, or out on any one of the home's three decks with the 180 degree view restored her strength. Gave her the energy she needed to be mother, entertainer, spiritual guide, provider.

Speaking of which, she needed to get back to her sewing room. A quick stroll to the end of the dock, and a dip of her feet into the chilly water and then she took the pine-needled path back toward the house. At the mid-level deck she slipped out of her water shoes, hosed off her feet, and dried them on the towel. She pulled her house keys from her pocket but when she reached for the slider it stood open about six inches.

Devynne's heart lurched and oxygen suddenly seemed elusive. She backed away from the door.

I locked it, didn't I?

Her gaze darted from window to window.

No lights on. Nothing on the deck seemed disturbed. Geraniums still on the rail. Marissa's sandbox still a scattered mess of toys. Only the door...

She pressed a hand to her thundering heart and forced a calming breath.

No forget that. There was absolutely nothing to be calm about in this situation! She spun around to flee.

A whisper of sound behind her. She gasped. Started to turn. But a sweaty palm clamped over her mouth and strong arms jerked her up tight against a hard wall of muscle and bone.

Not again! She swung her elbow with all her might and connected solidly.

The intruder didn't budge or make a sound. He only readjusted his grip so that her arms, pressed against her sides, cinched down within the noose of his grasp.

Her toes left the ground as he hauled her toward the open doorway. Terror surged, sapping her of the strength to fight.

Find out more about this series here: https://www.lynnettebonner.com/books/contemporary-romance/islands-of-intrigue-series/

Want a FREE Story?

If you enjoyed this book...

...You might also like *On the Wings of a Whisper*, a story set near the country where I was born and raised, Malawi, Africa. To start reading in just a few minutes, sign up for my newsletter below and the free book will be sent to you!

(My newsletter is only sent out about once a month or when I have a new release to announce, so you won't be getting a lot of spam messages, and I never share your email with anyone else.)

Here's a little about *On the Wings of a Whisper*...

Stone Town, Zanzibar, Early 1866

RyAnne Hunter is determined to stop her father from leaving for the continent of Africa, where he plans to start a mission station. And she only has until morning. Tonight at the Harcourts' Annual Ball will be her last chance to change his mind. She must succeed! Papa's health, and her future, depend on her success. But, as if her task isn't difficult enough, now the insufferable Captain Dawson has agreed to guide Papa's expedition!

After spending six months at sea, Captain Trent Dawson only wants to think about rest and relaxation. However, when he's recruited by a British naval officer to help put an end to a slave smuggling ring, the perfect opportunity presents itself in Dr. Hunter, who needs a guide to the Interior. Now if he can just help the doctor without spending too much time with the man's troublesome and flighty youngest daughter.

A thrilling historical romance from the time of missionary explorer David Livingstone.

This is part one of a six-part serialized story. Grab your free book here: https://www.lynnettebonner.com/newsletter/

About Author Lynnette Bonner

A former missionary kid who grew up on the sunny savannah and attended boarding school at Rift Valley Academy in Kenya, Lynnette currently writes from her home in the pacific northwest. You can find out more about her and her books on her website at: www.lynnettebonner.com.

If you enjoyed *Fire* and *Ice* in the San Juan Shadows series, you might also like my Islands of Intrigue series. You can find it here: https://www.lynnettebonner.com/books/contemporary-romance/islands-of-intrigue-series/

Also, if you would like, connect with Lynnette on Facebook here: https://www.facebook.com/authorlynnettebonner.

Made in the USA
Middletown, DE
18 June 2025